ECOTASTROPHE II
EDITED BY J ALAN ERWINE

Ecotastrophe II
Edited by J Alan Erwine

Cover design by J Alan Erwine

First printing July 2017

Nomadic Delirium Press
Aurora, Colorado
http://www.nomadicdeliriumpress.com

Contents

Editor's Introduction
By J Alan Erwine

More than a decade ago, Sam's Dot Publishing released a small anthology called *Ecotastrophe* that looked at futures on Earth where global climate change had been real, and the world had been ravaged by the effects of the changing climate. Now, more than a decade later, global climate change is still a very real threat to humanity...maybe an even greater threat, and Nomadic Delirium Press has decided to take another look at global climate change.

The stories in this volume look at several possible futures, some bleaker than others, and some looking at the grand scale of climate change, while others look at the smaller more personal consequences.

Whether you believe global climate change is real or not, I hope that you will at least enjoy the stories for the wonderful story telling abilities of the authors.

Enjoy *Ecotastrophe II*, and hopefully you'll help make a difference, and make sure that Ecotastrophe doesn't happen.

Gyroscope
By Tyree Campbell

Dear Towhomit,

I dove headfirst off the cliff this morning in what looked like a suicide attempt. A strong wind swept me up and deposited me back on the grass, several meters from the precipice. The others were aghast, of course; my father, especially. I'm the Heir to the Throne, so to speak. If there's going to be a Throne left. Why am I even here? It's my duty to

The flap to the tent opened. Without turning around, Paul Barrow knew it would be his father. He stopped writing and waited, knowing the old man would gather himself first, letting his anger steamroll into an outburst. But he closed the diary and placed the pen beside it. Waiting.

A faint whiff of something fragrant graced Paul's nose, and he realized someone else had entered the tent behind his father. Not his mother; she left discipline and recriminations to the old man. The only other viable options were Liza Talbot or her daughter, Alexandra Sinclair. Unless, of course, one of the men had a secret he was willing to reveal, now that the hunting party was isolated and lost. Alexandra, then, Paul concluded. But why?

His father cleared his throat, and muscles knotted in Paul's shoulders. At forty-four, the old man was not really that old, but he was so called around CommEarth corporate headquarters in Atlanta. Paul even referred to him obliquely as the old man, although a sneer sometimes accompanied the reference. After another coarse "ahem," the question reverberated throughout the tent like thunder.

"Just what in the hell did you think you were doing?"

Still Paul did not turn around. "I should have thought that would be obvious," he said, his soft voice a sharp counterpoint to his father's inquiry.

"You scared the shit out of me," said Barrow. "Your mother as well. What were you trying to do, kill yourself?"

Paul knew it would do no good to respond with the truth, but he made the attempt anyway. "I was trying to prove a point," he replied, and now stood up and turned around. As tall as his father's six-foot, but with far more brown hair, Paul had inherited most of his softer looks from his mother. Though he hardly looked effeminate, and certainly was nothing of the sort, his father continued to regard him as a creature of a weaker species. Even now, in the dim light of the tent, Paul felt the weight of his disrespect and disgust. You're *going to succeed* me *as president and CEO?* the old man seemed to be saying by his bearing and attitude.

Not if I can help it, Paul thought. But he had yet to summon the courage to say as much to him.

Behind Barrow and to one side stood Alexandra Sinclair, tall and slender and aloof. But now the expression in her dove-gray eyes was hard for Paul to read, in the shadow of his old man.

"And I suppose you're writing all this down in your journal," Barrow fleered, and wiped a sheen of sweat from his forehead with a dirty handkerchief. "Christ on a popsicle stick! What the hell would you have written, had you succeeded?"

The point was that I did not believe I would succeed, thought Paul. But he withheld the words, because they would only keep his father in the tent longer.

"It's a diary, Pop," he said instead, for the umpteenth time.

"Diaries are for sissies."

Paul's chest rose slightly and fell under the green jersey, his sigh inaudible. After a moment, silence won out. Barrow thrust the tent flap open and left, leaving behind a "Bah!"

Alexandra, to Paul's mild surprise, remained, tilting her head to one side as she regarded him with a curious expression. A smile toyed with the corners of her thin mouth.

"Am I in your diary, Paul?" she asked.

"No."

The smile died stillborn. "Oh."

Idiot, Paul told himself, after Alexandra ducked from the tent. We're stuck here, and she's the only female available for companionship. But the notion faded quickly; he had other problems to solve.

Sunlight heated Paul and brought forth beads of perspiration as he emerged from his tent. Along with his, the other four tents had been arranged in a circle, rather like wagons against natives in the Old West. Except they had yet to encounter any natives. He shaded his eyes and gazed out at the rolling savannah with its sparse, browning grass and its sprinkling of solitary trees; at the dense mixed forest on the hillside that bordered the encampment; and then, turning around, at the ocean beyond the cliffs and the narrow river that became a waterfall as it spilled down into it. The cliffs reminded Paul of the Cliffs of Moher on the west coast of Ireland, although these were but twenty feet high, if that. Near the precipice grew a copse of trees, and just landward of that rested what remained of the Cessna. The pilot, Roberto Dario, had been thrown clear and, presumably, over the cliff. They had not spotted his body in the rocks below—the rocks toward which Paul had dived head-first without success.

It occurred to him that he had no sense of direction in this place. He might assume that west lay in the direction of the sun's motion— the sun was in fact headed toward the horizon at the end of the ocean— but he had no confidence in that assumption. With a sliver of iron or steel he might contrive a compass of sorts, but they had not packed anything useful in that regard for a hunting trip. And the bag in which the compass had been packed was lost overboard along with the pilot.

Looking out at the ocean, Paul was aware of eyes on him, as if someone meant to prevent him from repeating his next death spiral. He turned his head slightly to look at the Cessna and the trees again. There on a boulder sat Adrian Skinner, who had been hired as the party's hunting guide. Skinner was in his early thirties, black-haired and pale-eyed, and generally as silent as the zephyr that filtered through the leaves of the trees. He had a lean physique, like that of a bicyclist or a climber, and of the men in the party Paul felt the least threatened by him. The eyes Paul had felt belonged to Skinner.

But it was a woman who touched Paul's arm. He twitched, and spun around, and found Alexandra standing within arm's reach. The heat from the sun was as nothing compared to that which now enveloped him, yet it was the heat from above which focused her attention.

"We should find shade," she said, "like the others."

"You're afraid I'll jump again."

Despite misgivings, Paul let her lead him to a cluster of trees opposite the Cessna and well away from the others. For the moment, at least, she no longer wore an air of superiority that verged on haughtiness; she seemed almost human now. He thought perhaps she was beginning to realize that, a week after the crash, they might be stuck here a while, wherever here was, and that her only other option for companionship was the taciturn man sitting by the airplane. But it was an act, a façade; to her he would suffice until they were rescued.

He did not tell her that he doubted a rescue was forthcoming.

They climbed a gentle slope and finally seated themselves on the trunk of a tree that had fallen to land at a slight angle, she a little above him, as if it befit her station. She was wearing what he surmised was the last of her clean clothes, a new pair of black jeans and an aqua pullover that exposed her already-reddened arms and shoulders. He was aware that she was not wearing a bra, and chided himself for even noticing. For even looking to find out. He switched gears, and wondered why she had brought him to this place, isolating them from the others. He was hardly attired to her standards; his own black jeans had worn through at the left knee, and the fabric over the right thigh was thinning. He'd worn the green jersey for the past four days. And his sparse, youthful beard was beginning to show.

"I'm sorry," she said softly.

"Only because of your limited options."

She stiffened. "You needn't be cruel."

"We should be clear where we stand, you and I."

"You've made yourself clear," she groused. "But can we declare a truce?"

"A truce," he said, without enthusiasm.

"An armistice, then."

Her voice trembled, and Paul glanced at her. A sheen of moisture made her pale eyes glisten. The budding tears might be real, or they might be a ploy. Suddenly he found himself wanting to trust her, and to trust what he saw in her.

"An armistice," he agreed, nodding. "Tell me why."

Alexandra hesitated, and dropped her gaze to the patches of grass between her feet. Paul had no idea what might shame her, and wondered whether her superior demeanor might itself be a façade. In a trice, she became to him a sympathetic creature—not weak, but burdened with normal human concerns exacerbated by their current plight. His right hand twitched; he wanted to reach out to her, to comfort her with a touch, but feared her interpretation of the gesture.

Her admission came out of nowhere. "Because I am alone, and I am frightened," she whispered.

Belatedly Paul understood. Two decades younger than most of the others, she'd had no one to talk to or to confide in. By nature distant himself, he had not encouraged conversation. Of roughly the same age, *of course* they should have gravitated together. He realized that now.

Sunlight through the foliage dappled her short golden hair, and tears still made her eyes gleam like silver in the broken shadows. He looked directly at her and said, "Cougar."

Startled, Alexandra blinked. Her lips formed a soundless question.

"You're five months older," he explained. "I won't make twenty-one for another month."

She barked a laugh. He thought it was good to hear her laugh, and better that he had made her do so.

"Tell me what frightens you," he suggested.

A brief silence followed, while she composed herself. "It's . . . little things," she said presently. "I . . . the day after we crashed, you looked up at the sky and said the sun was wrong. It was almost orange, and seemed smaller. My father said it was just pollution, like the horizon at sunset at Los Angeles. But that wasn't the sun, that was the clouds, and they were brownish orange. I've seen them."

"Wait till you see New Jersey. Such a lovely vermilion sky."

"Oh, I wouldn't want to go there." She brushed imaginary tresses from her cheek, and went on, "You also said this place was wrong, all wrong. I've been thinking about that. What did you mean by it?"

Paul did not respond

"Is this . . . are we on another world?" she asked.

"How could we be?"

"I don't know, I don't *know.* Our smart phones don't work. But the airplane's radio still works, and Adrian says it's not picking up any

14

transmission at all, not even static fuzz."

"Alexandra," he said, and paused. "May I at least save a couple of syllables by calling you Sandy?" he asked. *Or better yet, Alex,* he thought, annoyed with himself, *but it was already too late to change.*

At first she frowned, almost glaring at him. "Just not in front of the others," she relented.

"Sandy, you stayed awake during the flight across the Caribbean. Was the plane diverted? Did aliens beam us somewhere?"

"You're making fun of me," she pouted.

"Not at all." He plucked a leaf from one of the trees and examined it without interest. "The truth is, I've had parallel questions. But no answers. Thus my comment about something all wrong."

They heard a shout. John Talbot was returning from what he called a recce, a term from his few years in the military. A plumber by trade, he had improved his lot in life when he became Barrow's hunting partner. He was carrying a fabric shopping bag from which protruded a long branch, and he was waving for attention. "I found berries," he declared.

"Oh, good," said Paul, *sotto voce.* "We can eat."

Alexandra laughed, but added, "We'll need to arrange a food supply if we have to stay here much longer."

Paul stood up.

"Where are you going?" she asked.

"I want to look at the ocean again," he told her.

Her eyes widened. "You're *not* . . ."

"No, of course not." He held out his hand, and she took it, pulling herself to her feet. "I want to check something."

They strolled toward the precipice, and halted when they were able to see the rugged shoreline below. It stretched in either direction as far as they could see. Directly below, the waves worried at clusters of dark rocks that had fallen from the cliff in years and centuries past. Salty froth flew almost high enough to reach them.

"No wind," said Paul. "Wind kept me from falling, but now there's not even a breeze."

She touched his hand, and took it. "But what does it mean?"

"All in all," he said slowly, feeling his way, "it means we are

15

marooned here by design."

"Seriously. By whom? Why?"

Paul noted that she took his remark at face value, without the sarcasm he was accustomed to from his father. He shook his head. "I don't know. I do know that I should have fallen onto the rocks." He turned to her. "On the way, we flew west of the West Indies; that was the flight plan. You were looking out the window. Did you see a volcanic cloud? A plume forty thousand feet high?"

"N-no. What . . . ?"

"Because Pelee on Martinique had been erupting for the past four days."

She shot him a worried look. "But what does it mean?" she asked again.

"It means we never made it to Guyana." He glanced around. "I don't know where this is. Somewhere within fuel range. Colombia, maybe."

"Not another world?"

Paul felt helpless against the question. A misdirected flight? Another planet? Either way, he had no facts to tell him how, or why. All he had was a sun that looked odd, and a gravity that could be neutralized by wind. And a volcanic eruption that had not been spotted. He told her as much.

"A radio that works but doesn't seem to reach anyone," Alexandra added.

"We've been brought here for a reason," said Paul. "I think I proved that harm will not befall us. It won't be allowed."

"It sounds like a *Survivor* episode."

Paul chuckled. "That's easy enough to disprove. You're not wearing a bikini."

"I didn't even bring one."

"Well, darn."

A voice called to them. His father's voice. It boomed enough to frighten seagulls, Paul thought . . . and stared out at the ocean again. Where were the seabirds? He added that to the list of Odd.

"Coming," he called, and led Alexandra back to the others.

*

The gathering—Paul could hardly call it a meeting—was run by his father, Marcus Barrow, CEfuckingO. It consisted of announcing a decision made without Paul's input, or Alexandra's, either.

"We are marooned and incommunicado," began the elder Barrow, without preamble. "We don't know where we are. All this means we may be here for quite a while. We have supplies for twelve days—the anticipated duration of this hunting expedition—and seven of those days have already passed. We have weapons for our protection. We have shelter. We have clothing. We have running water of a sort. We can gather dry wood and make fire."

Barrow paused a moment to look at each person in turn. "What we do not have is a food supply. However, we have made a start in arranging one. Jack here has located a berry patch some distance away."

"About half a mile," Talbot threw in.

"He proposes to plant some canes around here," Barrow went on, "and I agree."

"That's a bad idea," said Alexandra. "Berry vines are very intrusive; they'll take over. We'll have to move our site before long."

"Which shows what you know, baby girl," snapped Talbot.

After a sharp glare at the girl, Barrow continued. "We'll start a rudimentary garden. We'll have to find things that are edible, of course. Other berries; nuts, perhaps some fruit. Game, if we can find it. Eggs—
"

"Do you see any birds?" Paul broke in. "Have you seen any here?"

"There are always birds, sonny," said Talbot, his tone dismissing the question. "We'll find them."

Paul shook his head slowly, but made no reply. Barrow said, "We'll all have to search for edibles. I want teams of two; in case one gets into trouble, he or she will have help." His gaze took in both Paul and Alexandra. "That includes the two of you," he added, directly to Paul. "It's about time you started to pull your own weight."

Alexandra's hand on Paul's arm soothed him. He decided to discount the notion of a façade; she was the girl she presented herself to be. He did not rise to his father's jibe. Instead, he stood up, and Alexandra with him.

17

"We'll go look for those edibles now," he announced, and they headed back toward the forest. He ignored the elder Barrow's snide remark about "*only* looking for things we can eat."

When they were out of earshot, Alexandra asked, "How long have you put up with that?"

"All my life."

After a moment, she said, "I hate my step-father."

"I agree with you about the berries," Paul told her. "But nobody's listening."

Trees forced them to make an erratic trail along the slope; they ducked, and pushed branches aside, and scanned the ground for anything that might provide some sort of nutrition. They found only sparse vegetation, leaves, and twigs. Here and there they lost their footing, and caught each other. Already, sweat dampened their shirts. From time to time Alexandra rubbed her bare arms, and Paul noticed that she had acquired several minor scratches during their walk.

"I think there's some aloe in the plane," he said.

"I hadn't planned on quite this much adventure," she admitted. "Mom and I were supposed to go shopping in Georgetown while the men were out hunting. Your mom was going with us." She smiled ruefully. "I suppose you were going with them."

"Reluctantly," he told her. "I've field-dressed a deer. I've no need to do anything like that again. And I haven't noticed any deer trails here yet, or any other trails, for that matter. No burrowing animals, no animal signs, no feathers, nothing."

"Let's add that to your list," she suggested.

"Already done." A breeze tousled his hair. "Hey, feel that?"

Alexandra's own short golden hair was already in disarray, and her loose aqua pullover was fluttering despite the extra weight of perspiration. "Where'd that come from?" she said.

Wind caught at Paul as he pulled Alexandra to the lee side of a broad tree trunk. "It actually reminds me of February in Chicago," he said. "Except this is a lot warmer. Sandy . . . I don't think we can go any further. This is about as strong as the wind that blew me back to shore."

Worry wrinkled her brow. "I don't understand."

He pointed toward another tree in the direction from which they

18

had come. "Let's go over there," he said, and curled an arm around her shoulders. "Hold onto me."

"Watch that hand."

He moved it higher on her shoulder. "Sorry."

"Don't be. You can try again tonight, and see what happens."

Again his face warmed, hotter than the sun, and remained so even as they took shelter behind the next tree. Here the wind lessened, gently soothing them, and she turned into the arm around her, and set her cheek against the top of his shoulder. He felt her breath heat the side of his neck.

"Thank you," she whispered.

"For?"

"This armistice. This . . . peace. I needed it."

His chin rubbed her forehead as he nodded. "Are you still frightened?"

"Yes. But it's all right now." He quickly put a little space between them, and she looked at him with a question in her pale eyes.

He felt his face flush. "Sorry."

Alexandra merely smiled.

"Let's follow a trail that runs along this wind," he said, leading her away. "We should find out how far it extends."

She trod carefully on loose dirt and past exposed roots. "Why?" she asked.

"Because I think the wind delineates our boundaries," he answered slowly, speaking the notion even as it occurred to him. "We're here by design."

"Nobody else will believe that," she said.

"And you?"

"I'm having some trouble wrapping my head around it," she conceded. "But . . . well, but. We have some facts, even if we don't know what they mean yet. And this wind is a fact as well. We don't feel it in the open, which is exactly where we *should* feel it." She paused briefly, the light breeze drying her skin. "Paul?"

He realized this was the first time she had called him by name. "Right here, Sandy."

"Whatever this is . . . whatever is going on here, I'm taking your part."

The declaration of faith lightened his heart. "Boom," he said.

*

The barrier of impassable wind continued all the way back to the cliffs. For the sake of direction Paul assigned the barrier to the southern boundary, the cliffs to the west, and the savannah to the east and north. A glance at the encampment suggested that none of the others had bothered to conduct a search. *Too busy making autocratic decisions*, he decided.

"Back to the war," Alexandra said quietly, as they approached.

Paul made a face as he spotted the berry cane and its dirt ball resting beside a hole already dug for it. Someone had cleared away the grass around it as well. Paul reckoned that, at a mere couple of meters from the Talbots' tent, the patch would compel them to move within two years at most. He doubted the time would matter—given the party had been brought here by design, the resolution surely would come within a reasonable time. Even so, the decision regarding the location of the patch was, to be polite about it, ill-advised.

But there was something besides dirt trapped in the ball, and as Paul drew nearer, he realized what it was. He bent down and retrieved a small, irregular lump of coal that had gotten wedged in the root system. *Something for his father's Christmas stocking*, he thought, straightening.

Almost immediately the elder Barrow snatched it from his hand, accompanied by a command to "Let me see that."

"It's coal," Barrow announced, having gained black marks on his hands. "Bituminous, from the look of it. If there's a seam, we can burn coal instead of wood. It burns longer, and provides more heat."

"Isn't it hot enough already?" asked Alexandra, with a glance back at the sun over the ocean.

Her step-father gave her a withering look. "For cooking, baby girl," he said.

"For metal-working as well," added Barrow. "Assuming we can find proper ores here."

"We won't be here that long," Paul muttered.

"We have to plan as though we will," countered the elder Barrow.

20

"Speaking of burning, we ought to plan a burn of some of this grass. It will add carbon to the soil, as well as clear a spot for a garden."

"You've no idea where the prevailing winds would blow the fire," said Paul. "You can't do this."

Barrow stepped closer, glowering. His torso puffed out the camouflage hunting outfit he was wearing. "*I* can't do this?" he snarled. "You forget who you're talking to, Paul."

For just a moment Paul started to square his shoulders and confront his father. But the moment passed, because Alexandra's hand on his arm reminded him that he had other concerns. Without a word, he turned around and walked away, with her still holding onto his arm.

"Come back here," shouted Barrow.

Paul did not even slow his departure. Presently he heard a sound of disgust, and knew that there would be no pursuit for his disobedience. He and Alexandra once again came to a stop where they could see the waves crashing on the rocks.

But there were no rocks below. The waves dashed against the cliff itself, barely ten feet below them.

Alexandra gasped, while Paul stood with his mouth agape. Madly he sought to reason out an explanation, but nothing occurred to him.

"What," said Alexandra, "does this mean?"

He took refuge in observable facts. "This isn't the Bay of Fundy," he said, with subdued confidence. "We're looking at an expanse of ocean, not a bay or strait where water can be channeled. The ocean level has risen about ten feet in the past . . . what, three hours? That can't be a tidal effect."

Worry and fear made Alexandra's voice shake. "So, in three more hours we'll all be under water?" she asked.

Paul shrugged. "If this were a natural phenomenon, there would be signs of inundation here. Yet we see none of that."

"So . . . something unnatural has changed?"

Now Paul sighed. "It would seem so."

"What?"

"I don't know." He glanced around. Already the rest of the hunting party was busy with camping chores. All except Adrian Skinner, the guide who was now seated on the airplane's broken wing, and Skinner was watching him and Alexandra. "I'm beginning to think he knows, though," said Paul.

"Shadows are getting longer," said Alexandra, her voice barely audible over the waves breaking below. "It will be dark in another hour or so. Paul . . . I'm hungry."

"*Delmonico's* is in my tent."

"Ribeye steak?" she said. "Baked potato with sour cream, broccoli with Béarnaise sauce, a merlot from Languedoc, and candlelight?"

"Would you settle for field rations, warm sodas, and a couple candles?"

"Boom," she said.

*

Dear Towhomit,

I am now convinced that we have been brought to this place, but I still don't know why. I now have an ally, and perhaps more: Alexandra Talbot

"Sinclair," amended Alexandra, hovering near his shoulder. "My father's name. I kept it. Alexandra Sinclair. Do you have to write that right now? I thought we—."

"Please. I need to do this while I'm thinking about it fresh."

Sinclair. We're developing a list of Odd, of things we know but cannot yet explain. We seem to be surrounded by an impenetrable wind, cause unknown. The ocean level is rising inexplicably; something must have changed in the environment, but what? I think Adrian knows

"No," said Alexandra. It was almost a yell. She began to walk around the center pole of the tent while she spoke her mind. "No, Paul, it's not that our environment is changing, but that we are changing our environment! Not us, not you and I. But the others. You've called them on it. Putting a berry patch here instead of simply gathering the berries when they're ripe. Burning the grass to clear a garden. Burning coal instead of wood. Planning to mine the coal, probably strip-mining, since the seam is near the surface." She paused to regard him. Already he had stopped writing, and was standing up where she wouldn't collide with him during her peripatetic thinking. "It's us," she said again. "*We're* changing it. *We're* the agents of environmental change."

Paul scuffed at the canvas floor of the tent. "You're saying that when we effect a change in the environment, the environment responds with a change of its own." Abruptly he rolled his eyes. "Well, duh! Yes, that's exactly what been happening, all over the planet. That's the simple equation. But . . . but these are local changes—the ocean level, the winds—and they must be engineered somehow."

Alexandra looked doubtful. "How would you engineer a ten-foot increase in the ocean level?"

"I don't know. Nuke Antarctica? But we've *seen* the difference in ocean level, Sandy. So it's happened. Or . . ."

She snapped her fingers. "Or it's all an illusion," she cried.

"I don't think so," he replied, shaking his head. "I think we really see these things—the ocean, the savannah, the forest. And certainly the trees are real, because they scratched you. But what part of what we see is real, and what part only looks real?"

A somber silence followed his question. Finally, Alexandra said, "This is crazy."

"A good night's sleep should help to clear our heads."

Her dove-gray eyes acquired a million-mile gaze. Her fingers toyed with the hem of her jersey, as if she were going to lift it. "What makes you think you're going to get a good night's sleep?" she asked.

*

"Captain Nemo," said Paul, the next morning, while they shared single-serving boxes of cold cereal. "He was the covert benefactor for the refugees who landed on his mysterious island. We're looking for Nemo."

"Adrian Skinner?" asked Alexandra, between crunches.

He shook his head. "He's the observer. I'm betting the radio does reach someone: whoever is behind this. They receive reports of what transpires here."

Alexandra dismissed this with a desultory wave of her hand. "Conspiracy theory," she snorted.

"Exactly."

She spun back around. "What?"

"We *are* the victims of a conspiracy," Paul went on. "To what end, I don't know, but—."

Shouts outside the tent interrupted him. Talbot's voice; something that sounded like a slap; a scream. His father demanding a cessation of hostilities, although not in so many words. Paul grabbed Alexandra's hand, and they rushed from the tent.

John Talbot was standing over his fallen wife, Alexandra's mother, who had a large red mark on her left cheek. He was so angry that he was unable to speak, and could only make mouth noises. The elder Barrow was tugging on Talbot's shoulder, trying to pull him away. Paul's mother appeared to be in shock. For a change, Adrian Skinner was standing up; he looked as if he might be about to intervene.

Alexandra rushed to her mother and knelt down on the grass beside her, arms around her for support.

Paul drew up to his father. "What's going on?"

"It's about time you woke up," said Talbot, to Alexandra. "You slut."

The vulgarity galvanized Paul in a way he had never known before. He stepped forward and swung his fist at Talbot's face. Though Talbot flinched, the blow landed on his cheek and knocked him back a step. Talbot caught his balance, and flashed a bloody grin as he raised his fists.

"Come get some, sonny," he said.

"That's enough, Jack," Barrow said, in a tone that demanded compliance. To Paul, he added, with only the barest hint of mockery, "Well, you might make a man yet."

Paul took a couple of deep breaths and let them out slowly. "What's going on?" he asked again.

"Liza Talbot has been sneaking additional rations," Barrow answered.

"I was *hungry!*" Liza screamed. Alexandra tried to hold her down, but she struggled back to her feet. "*Nobody* has done *anything* to get us out of here. It's all pioneer stuff with you. Ration this, ration that. It's . . . it's . . . *irrational!*"

"The radio doesn't reach anyone," Barrow said calmly. "We have to—"

"I'm not sure that's true," said Paul, with barely a glance in Skinner's direction. "I think we've received a response."

"You're crazy," sneered Talbot.

"What are you talking about?" Barrow demanded. "The radio doesn't get through. Our smart phones don't work. Nobody knows we're here."

Paul jammed his hands into his pockets and trudged over to the berry vine that had been transplanted the day before. Not unexpectedly, its leaves appeared to be somewhat wilted. He caught a whiff of something sour and pungent, and after several seconds he identified it. "Bug spray?" he said, turning around to address his father.

"We don't have any pesticide," said Barrow, with a trace of sarcasm.

Paul sighed. "Have you seen any bugs here?" he asked.

"No, but that doesn't mean they're not around. We can't take any chances with any crops we plant. And we're getting ready for that burn, so we have a place to cultivate whatever we can find."

Paul shook his head. "The prevailing winds blow out toward the grasslands. If you start a fire here, there's no telling how far it will burn out of control."

"We'll control it," Barrow said, his jaw clenched. His eyes flashed anger. "Same old Paul, trying to save the world."

"Just this little part of it. Pop, have you looked at the ocean?"

"Yeah. It's an ocean. So what?"

"Does it look a little different to you today?"

Barrow squinted toward the horizon. Waves were dashing above the cliffs, with the wind blowing salty spray inland. "Tide's come in," he said at last.

Paul held out an ushering arm. "Let's go up and look at it," he suggested.

"I don't need to . . . oh, all right. I'll humor you."

They approached the cliff, with Alexandra trailing a step behind. None of the others followed, but Paul had the impression that Skinner was watching them closely out of the corner of his eye. They reached a point about three paces from the precipice. Briny froth pelted them as the waves crashed not more than five feet below.

Staring, Barrow swore softly.

Paul said, "It's risen about fifteen feet since yesterday, Pop. That's not tidal."

"No," his father agreed.

"Tell him about the wind," said Alexandra.

"What about the wind?"

"The wind that blew me back onto the grass after I jumped," Paul replied. "The wind Sa . . . Alexandra and I encounter in the forest. It's a wall of wind, and it is impenetrable. It's as good as an electric fence. We tried, but we couldn't get through it." He looked back at the rolling savannah. "I'd bet if you go far enough out there, you'd encounter the same winds."

Paul paused for a moment, and took Alexandra's hand. "So what has changed since yesterday morning, Pop?"

The elder Barrow frowned. Wrinkles high on his forehead disturbed the gleam of sunlight from his balding head. "I'm not sure I follow you," he said. His gaze took in the pair of them. "Unless . . .?"

Paul held up their clasped hands. "I don't mean this," he said. "From the time we crashed here until yesterday, you were all plans and schemes and preparations for a stay of long duration. You were going to do this and that. But you hadn't actually done anything. Yesterday, you did."

He released Alexandra and began ticking his fingers as he made his points. "You dug up a berry vine and not only transplanted it, but you placed it in a spot not suited to this encampment. You sprayed it with bug spray without considering the effect that spray might have, on the plant *and* on the fruit it might bear. You're going to start a fire you probably will not be able to control—"

"You don't know—"

"*Will you please just for once hear me out?*"

For a moment, the elder Barrow's nostrils flared, as if he were on the verge of an explosion. With a visible effort he calmed himself, drinking in a deep breath and letting it out very slowly, while salty spray wafted all around them.

"You found a lump of coal and immediately planned to locate and exploit the seam," Paul continued, as if there had been no interruption. "You're going to use it in our campfire instead of harvesting the fallen trees in the area and using them for firewood."

Barrow dismissed this with his tone. "You're concerned about carbon emissions."

"The *point*," Paul said stiffly, "is that you're *not*. The point is that you glommed onto the idea of burning coal as soon as the opportunity arose, yesterday, without at least exhausting the alternatives first. And the main point is that this occurred *yesterday*."

"I don't care for the way you're talking to me, Paul," said Barrow.

"I don't care for the way you never even grant me the courtesy of a hearing, Pop."

Alexandra inserted herself between them, her presence a silent plea for peace.

"Right," said Paul. His lips puffed as he blew air out. "I'll just finish. Half a minute. You can wait that long to resume raping the landscape."

Alexandra's hand on his arm stopped him.

Paul nodded. "But see, that's what has changed, Pop. Since yesterday, you've either taken action or made specific, deliberate plans to take action on our environment here. Since yesterday, the ocean level has risen," he glanced out at it, "a good fifteen feet. Now, I'm not prepared to explain why this has occurred; I know only that it *has* occurred, and that it has occurred in apparent conjunction with the various actions I listed."

"Apparent," repeated Barrow.

"I'm guessing that if you continue changing our environment," said Paul, "the ocean level will continue to rise, flooding our campsite, flowing up that river over there and inundating the land."

Barrow made a sound of disgust. "What you're suggesting isn't even possible."

"What if it is?"

"Then tell me how," demanded Barrow. "You're suggesting that my decision to burn coal in our campfire has caused the ocean level to rise fifteen feet." He looked sharply at Paul. "Do you understand how insane that sounds?"

"In fact, I do," said Paul. "But humor me a little longer. Go back to the camp and tell the others that you're not going to burn the grass or spray any more plants with Bugdead, and you're going to harvest and burn firewood for cooking and for warmth." He looked up at the sun for a moment. "Though why we need warmth here, I've no idea. Anyway, go tell them. It's only noon, or close to it. Let's see what happens to the ocean level by sundown. If it has gone way down, will you at least give my thoughts some consideration?"

Barrow turned away and headed back toward the camp.

"Pop?" called Paul.

But the elder Barrow waved him off, and continued onward.

*

"What are you thinking?" asked Alexandra, after Barrow was out of earshot.

"It's a set-up," Paul answered. "I don't know how, and I'm not completely sure why, but someone is trying to teach us something. More specifically, to teach my dad something." He looked out at the ocean again. "It's the only thing that makes sense. And even that doesn't make sense."

"But you got him to listen to you," Alexandra pointed out. "That's something."

Paul turned and glared at the camp, where his father was talking in a low tone to the others. "He's probably telling them to go out and bring back all the coal they can find."

Hand in hand again, they began walking toward presumed north and the river. Paul drew his concerns away from the environment to give some attention to what had developed between himself and Alexandra. Something of an outcast in the camp because of his tender age and his father's general dismissal of him as a sentient being, he was grateful that Alexandra, Sandy, was taking his part whenever it seemed necessary. They'd formed a bond under the duress of isolation, and the romantic in him wondered how long that bond would last after they returned to civilization.

"You're awfully quiet," said Alexandra, as they reached the crest of a low hill that marked the halfway point to the river. She squeezed his hand. "But you're not tense," she went on. "So you're not thinking about your dad and what he might do. Therefore, it's either the problem of why we're all here, or . . . or it's about us. You and me. I'd say a penny for your thoughts, but inflation is rough these days. How about two dollars and fifty-three cents?"

Paul smiled in spite of his questions.

"That's better," she said.

"This is sudden and unexpected," he blurted, unable to stop himself.

"Maybe for you."

He stopped, and turned to her. "What does that mean?"

"I'm not as impulsive as it seems," she admitted. "Since this trip began, I kind of knew you and I would . . . okay, maybe not last night in your tent, but I thought at least we would get better acquainted. I mean, we've known each other for years. But you appeared to be more interested in your diary."

"It's therapeutic," he told her, as they resumed their journey toward the river. "And cathartic."

"I shouldn't wonder."

"It helps me keep myself together whenever I feel like I'm coming apart."

"You don't want to follow in your dad's footsteps?"

"God, no. I want . . . I want to finish up my degree this semester and . . . and . . ."

"Save the world?" she asked.

He shook his head. "That's not a task for one person," he said. "No, I just want to do some good, somewhere."

"Greenpeace? Quietearth? Sierra Club?"

"Yeah, maybe."

They reached the final downward slope before the river, and swished through the sun-baked grass. "Ah, skinny-dipping," she said.

The notion startled him. "What? No!" He felt his face warm. "I mean, no, that's not why I wanted to come here."

"Pity, that."

"Besides, they might see us. No, I wanted to find out how far we could go in this direction."

"About as far as we went last night in the tent," she said smugly. "If we stay below the crest of that last hillock. Paul?"

"Yeah?"

"Just kiss me, and I'll shut up. I know you've got a lot to think about. But you don't have to worry about you and me, about *us*." She clutched at his hand again for emphasis. "Understand?"

"I do."

"One more thing," she said. "I love the way you are so gentle with me. But every once in a while, I'd like you to keep in mind that I'm not made of spun glass. I won't break."

"Um," he said. "I, ah . . . to borrow from double-o seven, you want to be taken, not interred."

She groaned, then glared at him. "That was an unspeakable pun. You are *so* going to pay for it. Now, shut me up."

He kissed her.

"You can do better than that," she pouted.

He could, and he did.

*

The river purled past them, on its way to the ocean. Though the dusty yellow-orange sun had sunk halfway down to the horizon, it cast enough heat on Paul and Alexandra to keep them perspiring well after they had finished causing themselves to sweat. Sprawled now on the makeshift bed of their clothing, they each fell into their own reveries. Paul's, to his chagrin, focused not on the young woman beside him, but on their current plight. He felt as if there were some essential ingredient that continued to elude him; that if he could identify it, everything here would suddenly make sense.

Someone, Paul was certain, had managed to control a little portion of the environment. Or had established the semblance of control. The hunting group had intruded—or had been made to intrude—into this portion, and to affect or plan to affect that control. Their actions were akin to jamming a stick through the spokes of a moving bicycle.

"Gyroscope," Paul said suddenly, and sat bolt upright, startling Alexandra. Her dove-gray eyes peered up at him, squinting in the sunlight.

"The environment here is like a gyroscope," he expanded. "We've been sticking things in the spokes. It's off-kilter."

"The environment anywhere," Alexandra put in. As unselfconscious as Paul, she sat up and drew her knees up, wrapping her arms around her legs. "I think I see what you mean," she went on. "In the past two days we've made adjustments to our surroundings, all of them without giving any thought to the effects those adjustments might have."

Paul nodded. "There's nothing inherently wrong in planting a berry vine bramble for cultivation and harvesting," he said, more thinking out loud than speaking to her. "But we planted ours without planning, without asking ourselves what it would do to our surroundings. We sprayed it with a quasi-insecticide without asking what it would do to the ground, to ourselves, and to our digestive systems. We're going to burn the grasslands to make room for crops. Crops which in fact we don't even have seeds for. We're going to burn coal unnecessarily. Each thoughtless act upsets the balance of the gyroscope. Remember those toys we used to have as kids?"

"Um . . . no. But I know what one looks like," she added quickly.

"You could start them up by pulling on a string, like on a top, and stand them on the point of a pencil," said Paul. "No matter how you tilted the pencil, the gyroscope remained vertical. As long as it was spinning, anyway. A bicycle wheel is just another gyroscope, but on its edge. As long as you keep pedaling, the bicycle remains upright." He laughed, and said, "And so does the rider. But poke a stick through the wheel, and off you go. We've been doing that to the environment here."

Alexandra shook her head. "But that doesn't explain the rise in ocean level," she objected. "I mean, yeah, on a large scale, the things we do can affect it. They *are* affecting it."

"Pop's corporation has been quietly buying up land five to ten miles from the coastlines for years now," he said. "New waterfront properties. They'll be worth a lot more."

"That's sick."

"No, that's profit. I don't really blame him for that. It's a good financial move. But his corporation has also been doing things to the environment to *cause* those coastlines to change. In ignorance, I'm sure; Pop is neither malevolent nor malicious. Thing is, I doubt he'd stop even if he grasped the principle of environmental cause and effect."

"But the rise in ocean level here," Alexandra persisted. "How does that fit in?"

"That," said Paul, "is a very good question. Maybe it hasn't actually risen."

"I don't understand."

"I'm not sure I do, either. I think it has to do with the mechanism by which they control this little portion of the environment."

"They?"

As if on cue, they heard Skinner's voice. It sounded close by, as if he were standing on the other side of the hill.

"Don't worry, I won't look," Skinner called. "But I would ask you two to get dressed now, please."

*

"I can't wait to read *this* diary entry," said Alexandra, as she climbed back into her jeans.

Paul chuckled, and fastened his belt. Her calling it a diary instead of a journal endeared her to him. She "got" him in ways no one else had done. But when they reached civilization again, what then? His face sobered as he looked at her. Insignificant for the moment were the personal problems he faced with his father, or their present isolation, even the strange man waiting on the other side of the hill to hear from them again.

Yet what did he really know about her? Like himself, she was in her last semester, he at Michigan, she at Wisconsin. He had been compelled to major in Business Administration by his father, but he had added a second major in Environmental Studies on his own, and in opposition to him. As far as he could recollect, Geology was her major, glacial geology her specialty. She had a second major, but it eluded his memory. Still, where did that leave them? He avoiding what his father declared as his duty by going off instead on a Greenpeace mission to save the blue whales? She at a post in Antarctica, studying glacial progression and calving?

"I thought I had put a smile on your face," said Alexandra.

"Post-coital lassitude," he told her.

"My, aren't we clinical."

Paul laughed, despite his mood.

"I told you not to worry about you and me," she reminded him.

"We can work this out." She paused, and added, flashing a grin, "Except on game day."

"Game day?"

"You're a Wolverine, I'm a Badger."

"Oh. Right." He gazed toward the crest of the hill and said, "We'd better see what he wants."

She tugged at his arm to stop him from calling out to Skinner. "What do *you* want?" she asked.

"Seriously."

"Yes, seriously."

"You," said Paul, without hesitation.

"Boom," said Alexandra.

*

They called out to Skinner that they were now presentable. The taciturn man quickly appeared on the crest of the hill and strode down to them. Seen up close, his long, ruddy face was darkened by a week's worth of stubble. But there was a touch of mirth in his pale eyes as he shook hands with Paul, then with Alexandra.

"We should sit down," Skinner suggested. "This may take a while."

The three of them moved to the river bank and made themselves as comfortable as possible on the rough grass. Paul was feeling a touch of embarrassment. How long had Skinner been waiting on the other side of the hill? What had he . . . heard? A glance at Alexandra told him she was asking herself the same questions.

"About two hours," said Skinner. "I heard what I needed to hear."

Paul started. Alexandra said, "Please don't tell me you're telepathic."

Skinner smiled. Paul thought it was the first time he had seen the man smile.

"Hardly," said Skinner. "But I'd be astonished if you both didn't have the same unspoken question, under the circumstances." He leaned back on the grass, arms braced behind him. "You've almost put it all together, Paul," he went on, adding with another smile, this one directed at Alexandra, "with some very good insights from you. I particularly enjoyed the gyroscope analogy. Most apt. What you two are seeing—some of what you're seeing—is holographic. You've

33

already located much of the boundary. The remainder runs just on the other side of the river, which is real. Beyond that is actually a forest, much like the one next to your camp. The wind you feel is forced air circulating around the perimeter. As you've surmised, it is virtually impenetrable. We didn't want any of you to wander off . . . or to throw yourselves off the cliff. The sun's color is affected by the projection, By the way, on a lighter note, those berries tend to give you what we call the trots, as Mr. Talbot should be finding out fairly soon."

Alexandra laughed. Paul asked, "How are you generating the field?"

"It cost a bit of money, of course," Skinner answered readily. "We shut it off for a few hours each day in the early morning. The holographic generator is inside the plane, which is why I generally discouraged anyone from going in there. Especially you two."

Alexandra's pale brow wrinkled. "Why us?"

"Because *we* were the targets of this exercise," Paul said suddenly, having just made a connection. "Not my dad, or yours."

"But why?"

Paul looked to Skinner, who said, "You can lead a corporate executive to the truth, but you cannot force him to accept it. A nice little truism. 'Nice' in its original meaning, that is to say. To your father, Quietearth is just another radical fringe organization bent on pelting various upper management individuals with spoiled cabbage and tomatoes." He laughed lightly, and went on, "Not that we haven't done that, but there are those of us who realize that to elicit a lasting and useful response, we have to have both demonstrative proof and a rational program. You can't just shut down refineries, or EMP every vehicle that has electronic ignition—which is just about all of them these days—or stop mining coal. Nor should you want to; there is a happy medium that can be reached. There are those of us at Quietearth who are working on relevant proposals based on our independent studies. In the meantime, someone needs to . . . let's say 'cultivate sensibility' in the minds of those who have the power to effect change quickly enough to do some good, yet slowly enough to cause no more than the maximum acceptable disruption. Obviously, that's a fine line to walk."

"You said 'someone,'" said Alexandra. "Not Quietearth, then?"

Skinner turned to Paul. "Would your father give us a hearing?" he asked.

"He wouldn't want you in the same zip code," replied Paul.

"But he might give Paul a hearing," Alexandra cried suddenly. Her face glowed with her eureka moment. "*That's* what this is all about."

"Especially," added Skinner, "if you have something simple and demonstrable to show him."

"Like the rise in ocean level," said Paul.

"And the fall of it," Skinner put in. "Before I came out here, I listened. He wasn't happy. But he told the others they were going to hold off on the burn, and use fallen trees for firewood. He even got his wife to wash off the leaves of the berry vine, not that that will make the berries more edible. That's not the point."

"So the ocean level is," began Paul.

"Part of the illusion," said Skinner. "Oh, there *is* an ocean there. You felt the spray. But it's about twenty feet below the cliff. And the projection will show that presently."

"How," said Alexandra. She licked her lips and tried again. "How did you manage all this? I mean, holograms and . . . illusions and who knows . . . ?"

A faint smile toyed with the corners of Skinner's mouth. "We had a lot of help from some folks in Marin County," he admitted. "Of course, it helps that we're now a tax-deductible organization."

"Where exactly are we?" Paul asked.

"Near Punta Herrera, on the Yucatan coast. No, you would not have spotted the volcano smoke."

"Omigod," cried Alexandra. Her eyes widened in horror as she regarded Skinner. "You got the pilot killed, just to set this up. You're a—"

Skinner quickly shook his head. "We've taken great pains to keep all of you safe," he told her. "As Paul here learned first-hand. No, Roberto Dario is very much alive. He's not just a pilot, he's a stunt pilot, and a very good one. Works for indie films, mostly. He knows how to crash. You'll see him again when we reach our support camp, about half a kilometer beyond the wind barrier." He looked from Paul to

Alexandra and back again. "Well, *someone* has to fly you out of here."

*

"An illusion," said Barrow.

He and Paul were standing near the precipice that overlooked the ocean, with the sun about to set. Twenty feet below them, waves continued their slow erosion of the rocks.

A lesson, corrected Paul, thinking to himself. It would not do to rub his father's nose too hard in the mess he had made. Little steps, Adrian Skinner had said. We're in a hurry, but we have time if we keep putting one foot in front of the other. This was a first step. One of many.

"A consequence, Pop," Paul said aloud. "A connection."

Barrow slowly nodded. "I'm beginning to grasp that. But you're suggesting that I close down CommEarth. That we close down the corporations—"

"No."

". . . and the manufacturing—"

"No."

". . . and millions of people will lose their livelihood—"

"No, Pop, that's not—"

Barrow turned to him and said softly, "Would you please just hear me out?"

Paul grinned. "Of course, Pop," he relented.

"What you're suggesting is a radical change that will destroy the country and society as we know it.Don't you like the life you have? Don't you appreciate your education, your car . . . your ribeye steaks?"

"I love ribeyes, Pop. I'm just not willing to use the Earth as a dump for animal waste, to say nothing of adding methane to the atmosphere, the smell of meat-processing plants located too close to the cities, the . . . I don't want to go on and on."

He gazed out at the real ocean.

Moments later, Barrow cleared his throat. "You seem to have cemented a relationship with Alexandra," he said, in the tone of a friendly observation.

Paul decided to be blunt. "If you're referring to last night and this afternoon," he responded, "that's really a small part of it. I keep a diary; you call it a journal. She calls it a diary. Not because it's a diary or a journal, but because it's what I call it. She accepts my frame of reference. She's compatible in ways I cannot even begin to express to you. Yes, there are differences. Education, university, upbringing. I can't imagine what it must be like to be raised by someone who is not your parent and who regards you as being in the way, as she has been raised. It makes me appreciate you and Mom, together all these years. But again, that's a little thing. Life is really a series of little things. Big things only obscure that.

"And what we do to the environment is a series of little things. A plastic milk carton here, a cigarette butt out the window there. Burning sulfurous coal because it's less expensive than anthracite. Manufacturing incrementally improved smart phones—like the ones your CommEarth manufactures in China."

"What's wrong with—?"

"The primary difference between the Polara 6 and the Polara 5 is that the Six accommodates ten—count them, *ten*—more apps than the Five. The Five accommodated sixteen more than the Four, which was geared to five hundred apps, or hundreds more than most people can keep track of. All three models came out in the past eighteen months. What a waste!"

"It makes money for us," Barrow protested.

"Yeah. Pop, it's not one thing and it's not just CommEarth. It's Red-Bands replacing Blue-Rays replacing DVDs replacing VHS—"

Barrow shook his head. "Technological development, that's all."

"Pop," sighed Paul, "we've had Red-Band technology since VHS came out. We just held it back to make more incremental money. But again, that's just one symptom. It's a lot of little things." He sighed again. "To fix it, we have to take one step here and one step there, so their effects accumulate like a downhill snowball. No, we can't shut things down. Yes, the end result might well be the radical change that you fear so much. But that's a couple centuries or more into the future. It's a big change, but over time people will adapt. If we do things right, the effects of most incremental changes will be minimal. You won't realize you've traveled until you arrive at your destination."

His father, uncharacteristically, did not respond.

Maybe he's mulling it over, Paul thought. It's a beginning. Now to get him involved . . .

"Pop, you're worth six billion dollars. People will listen to you."

Barrow stared at him. "*Seven* billion, thank you."

"I know." Paul faked a downcast look. "I was kind of hoping for an allowance."

Incredibly, Paul felt his father's arm slip around his shoulders. They began walking slowly back to the encampment. "I was thinking more along the lines of a wedding gift, if it comes to that. Or perhaps if you had it now, it might lead to that. What would you do with it?"

Paul shrugged. "Set up a trust fund to disperse it where it's needed."

"Always the sensible one. You are going back to the university, right?"

"I have to keep up with Sandy . . . I mean Alexandra."

Barrow stopped, and Paul with him.

"As for people listening to me," Barrow said. "I do know two or three senators who are up for re-election next year. And . . . other people."

"Seriously."

Barrow nodded. "I won't say I'll agree with everything you think, Paul. But it might be useful if you formed some sort of consultancy, to advise me on where we should and should not develop. I might not take the advice; in fact, it's doubtful that I will. But . . ."

"But it's a little step," said Paul. "And CommEarth would be leading the way."

Barrow grinned. "That thought had occurred to me."

Alexandra spotted their return, and walked out to meet them. She disengaged Paul from his father, and led him aside.

"Did you two have a nice talk?" she asked.

"He thinks I should start an environmental consultancy for corporations," Paul answered. "I think I agree."

Her eyes brightened. "Want some really really long-term help?"

"Boom," said Paul.

Kale
By Dan Rice

I was born in 2035, the year the last gas-powered car rolled off the assembly line. That was the second year of The Great Drought, although no one living in the Pacific Northwest expected the well below average rainfall to stretch on for nearly two decades. By the time I turned eleven, the drinking water supply for Western Washington had been at critical levels for five years.

That spring Mount Rainier's once mighty glaciers withered to skeletal fingers. Rivers fed by unprecedented glacial melt flooded. By late spring the high waters receded and by the summer streams were dry and rivers were drying up. That year the Legislature enacted the Water Conservation Act, resulting in limiters installed on every residential water meter in the state and, among other things, made showering more than once a week a crime. Yeah, the B.O. got pretty bad.

When June of that fateful year rolled around, I wanted school to be over. The air conditioning failed two weeks earlier, making the classrooms stiflingly hot. The teachers opened the windows, propped open doors, and brought in fans, but those measures didn't stop me from sweating until my shirt stuck to my back.

"Maybe we'll have class outside tomorrow," I told Gwen, my classmate and best friend, as we walked home after school down a cracked sidewalk that radiated heat. "I heard Mrs. Collins taught her class outside."

"Jennifer told me that Nate Dryer got a bad sunburn yesterday and his mother called the school," Gwen said. "The principal visited Mrs. Collins today. No more classes outside."

"Well, shit," I said, quoting a phrase I often heard my father use. "Only Nate Dryer is dumb enough not to wear sunscreen."

I kicked a pebble down the sidewalk. The small stone skipped over the concrete and came to a rest on the dusty yard of a run-down house with white paint peeling off the siding in long jagged strips.

"I don't like it when you curse, Theo."

"Sorry," I said. Sometimes Gwen sounded like my mother.

"Nate isn't stupid. He's just poor. Jennifer told me he's on reduced lunch."

"Did your dad finish xeriscaping your backyard?" I asked, anxious to change the subject.

"He did," Gwen said, her eyes sparkling. "Do you want to see? I know. We can do our math homework together at the table. Don't worry, there's an umbrella to keep the sun off us. You'll love it. It's fab."

"Sure. That sounds great."

We turned off of 12th Street onto North Monroe. Gwen lived half a block up the street and my house was one block beyond hers. We walked in silence, just enjoying each other's company. That's one thing I always liked about Gwen, the silences between us were never uncomfortable.

Most of the yards were xeriscaped, basically gravel sprinkled with a few drought resistant cacti, and the modest houses were kept up. A good middle-class neighborhood, well-to-do compared to most of the city. Manicured trees used to line the road, but the drought killed them a couple years ago.

"Hey, Theo Four-eyes, Gwenny Penny, wait up. We want to talk to you."

I groaned, recognizing Dale's voice. I wanted to run, but after a quick glance over my shoulder I realized Dale was too close for us to escape. Behind him trailed two Neanderthals that followed him everywhere like loyal mutts. All three were big and wore sweat stained t-shirts.

Gwen assaulted them with charm. "Hi. Did you all have a wonderful day at school?"

I stood my ground with Gwen. The Neanderthals looked surprised to be politely addressed, but Dale remained unfazed.

"I need to tell you something about Four-eyes, Gwenny," Dale said, sneering at me. "Four-eyes' papa is a water hoarder. Ain't that right, Four-eyes? That's why your papa built that tall fence around his backyard. To keep people from knowing he's using water on that vegetable garden."

My face burned. I had heard these accusations from Dale before, but never in front of Gwen. Embarrassing. "Don't call me that."

"Don't call me that," Dale mocked. "He won't even deny it."

The Neanderthals snickered.

"Leave him alone," Gwen said, stepping between the bullies and me.

"You gonna make me, Gwenny," Dale said, unslinging his backpack and letting it fall to the ground. "You know, hoarding water is a crime. That's what my father says, Four-eyes. Your papa is a no good dirty criminal. He's gonna get caught and he's gonna be thrown in jail."

"You know what happens in jail?" a Neanderthal asked and made an obscene gesture with his hands.

Dale and his friends laughed. The Neanderthals playfully punched each other in the shoulders. I hung my head, so they wouldn't see the tears forming in my eyes.

"That's not true," Gwen said. "People are fined for hoarding water."

"Depends on how much water they steal. I betcha Four-eyes' papa uses...ummm..." Dale said.

"Gallons," a Neanderthal said.

"Yeah, gallons. You know what, Four-eyes? I'm gonna do me some investigating. I'm gonna find out what's going on in that backyard of yours."

"Come on, Theo, let's go," Gwen said.

Ignoring her, I glared at Dale. "Stay out of my yard. That's trespassing."

Dale just laughed. The Neanderthals joined in. Something about their laughter and the cruel mirth in their eyes enraged me. I charged past Gwen and shoved Dale in the chest with both hands. That stopped him laughing. He stumbled back a few steps almost tripping over his backpack.

"Pound him!" a Neanderthal said.

I started to sweat as much from fear as the heat. Dale was bigger than me, thick through the neck and chest. He clenched his hands into meaty fists. His right cross caught me on my bottom lip and dropped me onto my butt. My lip hurt like hell and I tasted blood in my mouth, but I refused to cry. I glared at him and the troglodytes he called friends.

"I'm calling my mother," Gwen said.

Dale grabbed his backpack. "Let's get out of here."

I wiped my lower lip with the back of my hand. It came away smeared with blood. Gwen helped me up. I basked in the glow of having stood up to Dale for the first time and having done so in front of Gwen. I convinced her to keep the encounter a secret. My boyish machismo didn't allow for tattling.

We went over to her house and I checked out the backyard, just like she said it was fab. My lip wouldn't stop bleeding and I worried that Dale might make good on his threat to trespass, so I soon headed home.

*

At home, I entered the bathroom and inspected my lip in the mirror. Blood coated my front teeth. There was a nasty gash on the inside of my bottom lip. I grabbed some toilet paper and pressed it against my lip to staunch the bleeding. I didn't want Mother to interrogate me when she arrived home.

Despite my effort, Mother remarked about my lip as soon as she saw me.

"It's nothing," I said, shrinking away from her attempts to check my wound.

"Theo, stop moving," Mother said and took either side of my head in her hands. She squinted as she scrutinized my injury. "Are you okay? You're going have a fat lip for a few days."

"I'm fine."

She released my head and placed her hands on her hips. "What happened?"

"I fell down. On the way home. Gwen and I had a race. I tripped on the uneven sidewalk."

"Tripped. Really?" Mother said, arching an eyebrow.

"My glasses slipped down my nose, you know from all my sweat. I couldn't see," I said, grabbing my backpack and heading for the stairs. "I need to do my math homework, Mom."

To my relief, I escaped to my bedroom that was a total disaster zone. I cleared some space in my desk and breezed through my math homework. Math came easily to me. That was one reason Dale and the Neanderthals bullied me. It was depressing.

Father's bellows summoned me to dinner. I smelled rolls as I descended the stairs. The rolls were great slathered in butter. The rest of the meal was unmemorable except for the fresh kale salad. The kale was from Father's vegetable garden that was illegal since outdoor watering was strictly prohibited. The dark green leaves were bitter and peppery. I couldn't take a single bite without screwing up my face in disgust, but experience taught me that I must eat the kale without voicing complaint or face Father's wrath. After dodging questions about my split lip and giving evasive answers about my day at school, I turned the questions on Father.

"Is it safe to have the vegetable garden?"

Father looked at me, eyes narrowing. He waited until he swallowed a mouthful of kale before speaking. "Safer than eating that GMO crap from the stores. Why? What's on your mind?"

"He's going to talk that way at school, Maddox," Mother said.

"Yes, dear," Father said. He looked at me expectantly.

"I heard at school you can go to jail for hoarding water."

"Jail? No, it's just a fine. $1,000, maybe. Anyway, our garden is no one else's business."

"You're sure?"

"Yeah, there's nothing to worry about. Screwing around with the water meter limiter will get you thrown in jail, but I'm not stupid enough to do that."

Mother leaned over and put a reassuring hand on my wrist. "No worries, Theo. Everything is okay."

But later that evening, when I was supposed to be in bed, I listened to my parents talking in the living room from my hideout at the top the stairs.

"You should pull up the garden, Maddox," Mother said.

"Why? I'll gladly pay the fine."

"People are angry and scared. Some of the things I hear at work. Talk about assaulting water hoarders. Arson."

"That's just talk. I hear that crap too."

"I'm serious, Maddox."

"To hear is to obey."

"I think Theo is being bullied at school. Maybe your garden has something to do with it. He's worried about you going to jail. I want that garden gone."

"I'll think about it."

After the encounter with Dale and the Neanderthals, I kept watch over the backyard before and after school. I set my alarm 15 minutes early, so after ravenously gulping down cereal and a glass of orange juice I could stand guard until it was time to leave. In the afternoon, I patrolled the backyard until Mother came home and forced me to scamper inside to do my homework.

On the third morning of my watchman duties, I woke extra early due to anxiety over a quiz that day. I wanted to shut my eyes until the alarm went off, but the urge to pee forced me up.

Downstairs I found Father's lunchbox and thermos sitting on the kitchen table. I noticed the sliding glass door was unlocked. Intrigued, I ignored my hunger pangs and went out the sliding glass door into the backyard. The cool air made me shiver. To the east the sun lit up the sky a vibrant pink.

The backyard was all dry dirt except for the large pile of gravel taller than a man to the left of the door. The gravel was for xeriscaping the yard, a job Father never seemed to get around to doing. I heard Father whistling *Ode to Joy* from behind the pile.

I walked around the gravel to where Father knelt beside his hidden vegetable garden, a 4 x 4 foot plot of loamy earth, pouring bottled water onto his leafy dark green kale. Next to him sat a half empty 24 pack of bottled water and a brown 10 gallon plastic sack about a third of the way full with what I presumed were empties.

"Dad, what are you doing?" I said, astounded he used bottled water on his stupid plants. "That water is for drinking. It's all over the media feeds. At school they told us all the bottled water is being shipped in from out-of-state."

Father looked up at me. "Keep your voice down. What's it look like I'm doing?"

"But -"

"Grab a bottle. Start at the other end."

I did as I was told, although I felt guilty. I learned at school that some people in the city didn't have enough water for cooking and a dozen homeless people had died from dehydration in the past month.

"You should pull up the garden," I said as I worked.

"That's what your mother says."

"Kids at school...they're on the lookout for water hoarders."

"That so. Good thing they don't know about our garden."

The water I poured onto the kale was meant for people not stupid plants. Yet here I was watering a vegetable that I hated. I felt terrible.

After the last drop of water fell onto a dark green leaf, I crunched up the empty bottle. "There's a boy at school, Dale, he knows about the garden from way back...he thinks we still have it."

"Dale? Do I know him?"

"Nah, we aren't friends. He maybe came over once or twice when I was in like kindergarten."

Father gave me a sideways glance and reached for the bottle I held. "Give me your empty."

I gave him the bottle. He silently stood and discarded both empty bottles into the plastic sack. He carried the sack and the remaining 24 pack to the crawl space access well alongside the house. After setting the bottled water and sack underneath the house, he placed the cover over the access well.

"Let's go inside," Father said. "I need to leave for work."

Before leaving, Father made me sit at the table and he sat down across from me. He stared at me for what felt like a long time. I bit my lip and fidgeted.

"Did you tell this boy Dale that we still have the vegetable garden?" he asked.

"No, never."

Father nodded. "Good. Then there's nothing to worry about. You probably wonder why I keep the garden with all these restrictions in place. There's lots of reasons. But there's one I want you to know. You're too young to remember your grandfather. He was a gardener. A damn good one."

My jaw went slack. I saw the tears well up in the corners of Father's eyes. He wasn't the crying type.

"He taught me to garden. How to tend living things, Theo. How to tend the earth. We can't let a drought make us forget that. I can't forget him," he said and fell silent.

"Dad, are you okay?"

"I'm fine, son. It's just…sometimes I wished you knew him, that's all," he said and took a napkin from the table to dab his eyes and cheeks. "I love you."

"I love you too, Dad."

He stood, grabbed his things, and left.

*

That day after school I walked home with Gwen. The burning hot sun made me sweat. It was embarrassing, Gwen didn't sweat at all.

"Theo, there's something I want to tell you," Gwen said. "During afternoon recess, Jennifer overheard Dale talking to his buddies. She said it sounds like they plan to vandalize someone's backyard today. I remember him threatening to break into your backyard."

"Today. Seriously," I said, starting to run home. Over my shoulder, I shouted. "Thanks, Gwen. I have to go."

I raced all the way home and arrived at the front door panting. Fumbling with my key, I dropped it on the porch. Muttering a curse, I picked it up and unlocked the door. I slammed the door shut and locked it. Running for the sliding glass door to the backyard, I paused in the kitchen long enough to pour myself a glass of water and gulp it down.

The backyard was torrid and dusty. I made a circuit around the fence line, checking for incursions. Not finding any sign of Dale or the Neanderthals, I marched behind the gravel pile to where the garden was hidden. I stared with hatred at the dark green kale with its purple stems. The temptation to rip the plants out tugged at me, but I feared Father's wrath. Maybe I'd just stomp one of the plants and leave it at that. I would have, but I heard metallic clinks followed by a loud banging.

I sprinted to the gate that was secured by a heavy-duty padlock. The gate shuddered. Someone tried to get inside.

"It's locked," Dale said.

"Maybe we can climb over," a Neanderthal said.

"I don't know. It's damn high," Dale said.

"We'll give you a boost," a Neanderthal said.

"Go away!" I shouted.

"Four-eyes? Four-eyes," Dale said. "Help me up, you idiots. I'm going to smash your face in, Four-eyes."

Shoes scraped against wood. The Neanderthals grunted and muttered expletives. Dale exhorted them to heave his bulky body up. I saw fingers grip the top of the fence.

"Crap," I said and ran for the gravel pile.

I grabbed a handful of good-sized stones and ran back to the gate. Dale's face poked above the fence. I took aim and chucked a rock, missing high and wide to the left.

"I'm going to end you, Four-eyes," Dale bellowed.

I looked at the rocks clutched my hand and choose one with sharp edges. I took my time aiming, concentrating on his broad forehead that was bright red from exertion. I threw the rock. It hit Dale just above the left eye. He screamed in pain and fell to the ground with a loud thud.

"I told you to go away," I said unable to keep the glee from my voice.

The Neanderthals asked Dale if he was okay. Dale cussed enough to make a truck driver blush.

"I'm gonna tell my father, Four-eyes," Dale said. "I'm gonna tell him what's going on in that backyard of yours. You're going to pay for this. Come on, let's get outta here."

*

At school the next day, Gwen and I received an award in front of the entire student body for placing first in a regional science fair. As we walked home, Gwen was effusive in her pleasure. She kissed me lightly on the cheek, her lips were soft and moist. I had never been kissed by anyone besides Mother. My heart thudded in my chest so hard I was amazed Gwen couldn't hear it and I blushed.

"You just have to come over and help me study for the math final, Theo," Gwen said after she kissed me. "You're still not worried about Dale, are you? I mean, you haven't seen him or his buddies around your house, right?"

I told her about Dale attempting to scale the fence and how I hit him with a rock.

"Oh, my gosh! Do you expect him to come back?"

"I don't know. He threatened to tell his dad."

"How about I come over your house? We can study there."

"Yeah, that's a great idea."

We studied at the kitchen table together. Gwen was good at math, but not quite as good as me. As I reviewed some of the tougher concepts with her my fear of Dale and the Neanderthals kept distracting me. Every so often, I'd go out into the backyard and look around. They never showed up.

*

The next morning, I descended the stairs still half asleep and was surprised to overhear Father chatting with someone at the front door. He should've left for work already.

"The kale is delicious, Maddox. Thank you."

"Enjoy it. Thanks for the water. I couldn't keep the garden going without it," Father said.

Curious, I scurried down the stairs and peered into the entryway.

"Hello, Theo," Eleanor said, a kindly elderly woman who lived across the street. She leaned heavily on a cane. She held a reusable grocery bag with kale poking out from the top.

"Hi," I said.

Father held a bag that I guessed was full of bottled water.

"Well, I know you have to be off to work, Maddox. You two have a good day," Eleanor said.

"You too, Eleanor," Father said and shut the door.

I wanted to question Father about the exchange with our elderly neighbor, but he brushed me off saying that he was late for work. Not too late to stash the bottled water underneath the house, but I knew better than to harass him when he was rushed.

*

The next week was finals and it went by fast. On Friday morning, flashing red and blue lights woke me up. The light came from outside and entered the room through the gaps in the blind covering the window.

Stumbling out of bed and putting on my glasses, I walked to the window and opened the blind. On the street, I saw two police cars in front of Eleanor's house. My father and Eleanor stood in her driveway. The elderly woman spoke to a police officer in a navy-blue uniform. Spray-painted in black across her garage door were the words 'U R DEAD WATER HOARDER'.

"Oh my God," I said.

My upper back and shoulders tightened. I burst from my room and sprinted down the stairs. Dressed only in boxers, I pulled open the sliding glass door and darted out into the backyard. Despite the early hour, the dusty earth warmed the soles of my feet. The glare of the sun made me squint.

As I rounded the gravel pile, my panicked mind formed a plan of action. I would tear up the kale with my bare hands and cover the loamy earth with gravel. I would stash the kale beneath the house for the time being and properly dispose of it later.

"What?" I said stupidly as I came to a halt behind the gravel pile.

Gravel covered the garden. I dropped to my knees, pebbles digging into my skin, and scooped away the rock with my hands. I feared he pile had shifted on its own and buried the garden and that the damning evidence was still there to be discovered. I found nothing, not even a handful of loam. I checked the crawl space for evidence. Nothing. At the time, I assumed Father had finally given into Mother's demands. Years later I learned Mother had taken an afternoon off from work to dispose of the kale. She'd been scared by the experience of a coworker who had a brick thrown through a window of his house after being accused of hoarding water.

At school, I told Gwen my theory that Dale and his buddies vandalized Eleanor's house, but Gwen pointed out that they'd deface my house instead. After some debate, I decided Gwen was right.

*

During dinner that evening, Father declared he had purchased a handgun that very morning. The color drained from the Mother's cheeks and she stared wide-eyed at Father. Her fork, tofu impaled on the tines, slipped from her fingers and clattered against her plate. I was disturbed by the presence of a gun in the house too and her reaction increased my unease.

"Why?" she asked, her voice sharp.

"Protection. You saw what those thugs did to Eleanor's house. If they come around here, I'll have a surprise for them," Father said. "You don't need to worry about any accidents. I'll keep it unloaded and in a safe. Theo knows better than the play with a gun. Right, Theo?"

"Yeah, I won't touch it," I said. "But…maybe…maybe I should learn how to use it. Just in case."

"Theo," Mother said.

"I'll take you to the range," Father said.

"You make me sick," Mother said, glaring at Father.

Mother stormed off and stomped up the stairs. A door slammed.

Father shrugged. "She'll get over it."

I imagined I felt just as sick as Mother. I didn't want to learn how to shoot the gun. I only wanted to bait my parents, a social experiment to see what would happen. I never expected Father to take me to the range.

*

Before leaving for the range on Saturday Father showed me how to open the gun safe next to his bed. The code, punched into a keypad on the door of the safe, was the date of my parent's anniversary.

"Don't tell your mother about this," he said. "It's just between you and me. With everything that's going on in the city nowadays, this family needs protection. I won't always be at home. If I'm not here, you need to protect yourself and your mother. Got it?"

"Yes, sir."

As for shooting the gun, I hated it.

*

Sunday night Gwen and her parents came over for dinner. It was pretty nice, no kale. Despite the garden being pulled up, Father still had a stash in the fridge that would last for another week or so. But, Gwen and her parents didn't know that he had kept the garden going as an illegal enterprise. After the meal, the conversation turned to the goings on around town.

"Have the police caught the twerps who vandalized Eleanor's house?" Alejandro, Gwen's father, asked.

"No," Father said. "Eleanor has a camera by her front door, but it didn't catch anything. Neither did mine."

"Too bad. God damn ne'er-do-wells," Alejandro said, his face reddening.

Piper, Gwen's mother, put a hand on her husband's wrist. "Your blood pressure."

"Daddy," Gwen said, her voice high.

"Calm down," Alejandro said, waving off their concern. "I'm fine. I took my meds."

"More red wine?" Father said, reaching for a bottle. "It will lower your blood pressure."

Alejandro cast a sideways glance at his wife and daughter. "No, thanks. It's this new blood pressure medication. I'm supposed to go easy on the alcohol. You know, these vigilantes really drive me nuts. Did you hear about the incident today up at Ruston?"

"No. What happened?" Father asked.

"Do you have to tell us about that at the table?" Piper asked.

"Come on, Maddox wants to know. I bet Theo wants to hear about it too," Alejandro said and winked at me. I vigorously nodded as expected. "An old dude, elderly, was beaten to death for hoarding water by his own neighbors. Skull caved in. Some punk decided to get in on the action and used a shovel. Can you believe it? He was stashing water to give to his dogs. Hoarding water is against the law and all, but that's not something to kill somebody over."

"What will happen to the dogs?" I asked.

"Euthanized, my man. City ordinance," Alejandro said, leaning back in his chair. "City doesn't have the resources to care for stray animals. You know, you're not even allowed to have more than one dog inside the city limits nowadays."

Across from me Gwen started to cry.

"Gwen, baby - " Alejandro said.

"You just couldn't keep your mouth shut, could you?" Piper said and wrapped an arm around her daughter's shoulders.

"What's wrong?" I asked.

"The dogs will be killed," Gwen said between sobs.

"Why?" I asked.

"That's what euthanized means, dear," Mother said.

"No. Seriously? That's horrible," I said, upset over the fate of the dogs and my friend's distress. "There must be like tons of people who'd love to take care of those dogs."

After Gwen calmed herself, we were excused from table to go hang out in my room. Once upstairs I told Gwen about the handgun and asked her if she wanted to see it. To my surprise, she did. We snuck into the master bedroom and I showed her the gun in the safe beside the bed.

"Your parents told you the code?" Gwen asked.

"My dad did. Mom doesn't know," I said and reached for the weapon.

Gwen grabbed my wrist. "No, Theo, I don't need a closer look. Thanks for showing me. Let's go play the VR."

"Okay," I said, shutting the safe. "Not as interesting as you expected, huh?"

"I don't know what I expected. Was shooting it fun?"

"Nah, just loud."

*

To my relief Monday was the last day of class. The temperature kept soaring higher and the school's AC still wasn't fixed. With the garden gone I didn't have a reason to stand guard over the backyard anymore, so after school I went over the Gwen's place and hung out with her until Mother came home. The short walk to my house under the scorching sun left me exhausted. After greeting Mother, I gulped down two cups of water and marched upstairs to my room to read an online fantasy zine.

Incessant doorbell ringing and banging disturbed my reading. Mother answered the door and I went back to reading about an old warlock and his dragon when angry voices echoed from downstairs.

Worried, I left my room and started descending the stairs. "Mom, is everything okay?"

"We know your husband is a damn water hoarder just like that old bitch across the street," a male voice, deep and angry.

I stopped on the stairs and grabbed the railing to keep my balance as my body quavered. My father wasn't a water hoarder, not anymore.

"Get off my property before I call the police," Mother said, her voice piercing.

My heart drummed a quick beat.

"We want that wa -"

The words were cut off by the door slamming followed by the mechanical click of a deadbolt sliding into place. The banging started up again then stopped. I lowered myself to sit on the stairs. Alejandro's story about the elderly man having his head bashed in played like a movie on an infinite loop in my mind. Only in my mind's eye, Father's skull cracked open like an eggshell when struck by the shovel.

My mother saw me on the stairs. She blinked back tears. "Theo, go to your room and stay there."

*

From my window, I watched five angry men mill about at the edge of the driveway. They were big. They were agitated. They were scary. The hair on the back of my neck stood at attention. I recognized Joe, a neighbor who lived a couple houses down and had always been nice to me. He didn't look friendly now.

When my father pulled up in his old hybrid, the men blocked the driveway. He stopped the hybrid in the street. He threw open the door and jumped out and exchanged words with the men. They surrounded him. Someone pushed him in the chest and another man shoved him in the back. A third man threw Father to the ground.

I heard the front door open and Mother scream. A man kicked Father in the gut. I felt sick to my stomach and helpless and so, so afraid. A wave of nausea swept through me and I looked away, unable to watch Father being beaten. When I look at the way, a mist parted in my mind. I wasn't hopeless. I knew how to use the gun in my parents' bedroom.

*

I ran outside past Mother who screamed into her phone. In my peripheral vision I saw her reach for me, but I was too fast.

"Theo! No!" she shrieked.

I ignored her. My gaze fixated on the men kicking Father. I raised the gun, aiming it toward the men.

"Stop!" I shouted.

Joe faced me, but the other men remained focused on Father.

"He's got a gun," Joe said, backing away.

"Leave him alone," I said.

53

The other men looked at me now. All looked afraid, except for one man who I recognized as Clarence, Dale's father.

"Theo, don't!" Mother called. "The police are coming. The police are coming."

"That's not even loaded, is it, Theo? My son told me about your old man being a water hoarder," Clarence said, sneering just like his son. "You just let us punish your father. You understand me, boy? Don't make me come over and take that gun from you."

Clarence advanced toward me. I pointed the gun in the air and fired then aimed it toward the men again. The color drained from Clarence's face and he fell onto his butt in his rush to turn tail and run.

"Jesus Christ!" Joe shouted. "Run. He's going to shoot us."

The men ran. Clarence scrambled to his feet and followed them.

*

A police drone hovered overhead, camera swiveling. A commanding voice came from the drone, ordering me to place the weapon on the ground. So scared I nearly peed my shorts, I dropped the gun. Mother sat beside Father, cradling his head in her lap.

When the police arrived, I was sobbing, certain that Father was dead and that I was going to jail. The low point was watching the medics put my unresponsive father into the back of an ambulance to rush him to the hospital.

Lucky for me, the camera by the front door recorded everything and I was heralded as a hero for saving Father from the vigilantes. Father suffered a concussion and broken ribs, but he made a full recovery and declares to this day that the handgun was the best purchase he ever made. The men who assaulted him were rounded up by the police within a couple of days and all spent time in jail for their deed.

Since that day I have never eaten kale again.

The Last Polar Bear
by Melanie Rees

From her warm den, she emerges. Even though it was a short winter, the sun is a stranger. Above the snow-speckled slopes, an enormous bird hovers. Its loud chopping squawk is like no gull, eagle or falcon she has ever heard.

She stands guard over her den as the strange bird flies over the white plains. The snow has already started to melt. Her stomach grumbles. No time to waste. It is time to feed.

*

The helicopter veered towards the chequered pattern of roofs flanked by snow. Aiden gripped the handrail, taking deep breaths.

"Look! Polar bear." Mick propped his sunnies on top of his head and peered out of the window.

"Where?" said Aiden, letting go of the handrail.

"Down there."

Aiden looked directly below. The roofs of the town were tiny coloured squares amongst endless white smothering the ground far *far* below.

Aiden clasped his mouth. "Oww! I think I'm going be sick."

"Polar bears?" The pilot had been silent during their journey but turned his head abruptly. "Didn't think you youngsters were serious?"

"Sure. Quick expedition before uni starts," said Mick. "We know we probably won't see one, but you never know."

"What! You mean there wasn't a polar bear down there?" Aiden growled at Mick.

"Sorry." Mick slapped him on the back. "Couldn't help it."

The pilot chuckled and took the chopper lower. Black Spruce bowed under the force as they descended upon the outskirts of town.

Aiden's boots sunk deep into the snow when he disembarked and the feeling of ground beneath his feet calmed his stomach.

"Here you are boys," said the pilot, hauling their hiking gear from the underside of the chopper and dumping it on the snow. "3D cameras, tranquilizer darts? You're optimistic."

Aiden ignored the pilot's goading tone and squinted at his

surroundings. Rusty train tracks peered through the snow; signs dangled from their hinges; shops were boarded up with planks; and between two train carriages, the lake glistened with a reticent gleam.

"It's awfully quiet," he said.

"Yeah. Tourism market crashed back in the 2050s. Don't see many folk travelling this far north no more," said the pilot, scooting back into his chopper. "But best of luck to ya. Polar bears," he muttered to himself. "Oh, my." The pilot laughed and took off.

Aiden and Mick ignored the pilot's lack of optimism and set off around the lake. Aiden walked in a daydream. The extended daylight hours played havoc with his sense of time but eventually the sun lost interest in the world. The glaring white plain became a silver glow and Midas came out of hiding and turned every rock and blade of grass to gold.

As they set up the tent, Mick pulled off his gloves with his teeth and positioned the camera next to the thawing lake.

"Glad you have your priorities right."

"Too right." He blew on his hands. "I want a time lapse of the stars." He put his gloves back on and retreated to the tent. "All we need now is some scotch and a woman to keep us warm."

"Sorry, didn't pack that." Aiden smiled and shuffled down in his sleeping bag.

Five seconds later, snoring resonated through the tent. "Mick!" Aiden prodded him, but Mick just grumbled.

Aiden wriggled out of his sleeping bag and wandered outside. The night air pierced his jacket and snow tumbled against his ankles as the wind suddenly intensified. It whistled across the lake with an indiscernible melody and lashed at his jacket. Aiden retreated to the tent, but as he did so, he tripped over the camera.

"Mick's going to kill me." He picked it up and scanned the images.

Flicking back through the photos, stars sailed in a semi-arc across the viewfinder and then there was a flash of white.

"Mick!" Aiden barely heard his voice against the howling wind. He returned to the shot and focused on the image. A white appendage? He clicked on the viewfinder and rotated the 3D image to look at it from another angle. A furry torso?

"Mick!" he shouted again.

Aiden heard his name echo on the wind. He spun in the direction of the voice, saw something white in front of his face and then everything went dark.

*

When Aiden awoke, springs dug into his back and a musky smell lingered in the air. Outside, the ocean roared; maybe he was back at his gran's coastal cottage. He craned his neck. Next to the bed, unfamiliar faces stared at him from a photo on the bedside table. A thick bearded man with a semi-toothless grin sat on the deck of a boat. Alongside him, a flaxen-haired woman held a blonde blue-eyed child on her lap. Next to the photo sat a silver locket, similar to his gran's. Disorientated, he propped himself up and opened the locket; it wasn't his grandmother looking back. Instead, a few fine strands of blonde hair were looped inside. This wasn't his gran's house. The roaring of the ocean intensified. Gingerly, he wandered across to the window. He peered between planks boarding up the window and saw the wind roar. Wind not waves. Wind... snow... blizzard.

He rushed towards the door. A teenage version of the white-haired child from the photo stood in the doorway. She was rugged up in a white jacket and thick white gloves. With her platinum blonde hair, she looked like an angel.

She pointed down the hallway. Aiden followed her directions. Dusty photos in chipped ornate frames covered the walls: mountains of white, seals and countless landscapes. Beautiful photos neglected and decomposing.

The hallway opened up into a large dining room and kitchen. A fireplace crackled nearby. The scenery was homey, yet the furniture derelict.

Mick and an old man sat at a huge wooden table. Bread and cheese were laid out before them.

"You 'ook 'ike crap," Mick said with his mouth full.

"Ursula, find another chair," muttered the old man.

Ursula hurried back down the hallway.

The man reached across Mick and grabbed a chunk of bread from a fresh loaf. "Better get some before your friend eats this month's

57

rations."

Ursula tapped Aiden on the shoulder and offered a chair. Her white hair shimmered in the light of the fire.

"Thank you."

She looked down shyly and stepped away from the table.

Aiden touched his swollen lip. "What happened? Where are we?"

"Dr. Foreston brought us back to town in his Tundra Buggy." Mick nodded towards the old man.

"So, we're safe. The polar bear isn't going to attack us here?"

Dr. Foreston grunted, spraying breadcrumbs across the table. "Polar bear! Hah, not likely. Even if there were still some alive, they wouldn't look at you twice unless you were a plump hundred pound seal."

"I saw one. Well... I saw something... on the camera."

"Nothing attacked us," said Mick.

"What, I just fell did I?"

"It was just a late winter blizzard. The tent pole probably hit you. It went flying when the winds hit. Ripped the tent apart," said Mick.

"But I saw something white before I fell."

"Saw something white? Out here? In the snow? Couldn't be." Mick smiled.

Aiden rolled his eyes. He looked at the old man: unkempt hair, rugged and abrupt. A stark contrast to the young and reserved Ursula. She wandered around the kitchen tinkering with dishes. She turned and for a moment, he saw glimpse of a tight-lipped smile.

"Aren't you eating?" Aiden asked.

Ursula clenched the china plate she was holding in her gloves, her eyes dancing nervously between the faces at the table.

"She can have her supper later. Now it is time to do the dishes. *Isn't it,* Ursula?"

She stared with pleading eyes and then retreated to the kitchen.

"That's a bit harsh," said Mick. "You can't keep her secluded from the rest of the world. It's so isolated out here."

"Don't tell me how to raise my daughter. I've raised her myself and she's fine."

Mick slumped in his chair and drummed his fingers on the table.

"Where's her mother?"

"Boating accident," Dr. Foreston kept his eyes firmly fixed on his food. "Ursula nearly drowned too."

Mick looked at Ursula. "I'm sorry."

"So what are you doing out here, Dr. Foreston? Are you the local GP?" asked Aiden, changing subject.

"No." Dr. Foreston glared. "I was researching arctic wildlife. Genetics and climate change adaptations, that sort of thing."

"Arctic wildlife?" piped up Mick.

"Beluga whales, polar bears, and other threatened species."

"So you'd know the best place to spot polar bears?" Excitement prickled Aiden's skin.

Even Mick stopped eating.

"*Was* researching. Past tense. I haven't seen one in years."

Aiden cradled his head deep in thought. "You must've seen one. You're here all the time." He looked up when Dr. Foreston didn't reply. "There were reported sightings. Sure, they might be elusive, but—"

"There are no polar bears. You made sure of that," Dr. Foreston interjected.

"What! What have we done?" Mick stiffened.

"You... you're all the same. Driving your gas guzzlers, living in your square city cubes. Don't worry if you melt my home, you can always just turn up the air-conditioning back home."

Mick stood up, grating his chair on the floorboards. "Steady on."

Dr. Foreston stormed out of the room. "Frequent flying fools, getting stuck out here..." His voice trailed off as he retreated down the hallway.

"Okay," began Mick. "He's clearly a raving loony."

"Keep your voice down." Aiden spotted Ursula. She stood in the kitchen, unresponsive, focused on the dishes. "Poor girl."

"Don't even think about cutting my lunch again. I saw her first," jibed Mick.

"Really!" said Aiden. "We almost died and you're trying to pick up?"

"We didn't almost die."

Mick looked at Ursula as she approached the table to collect dishes.

"Do you want a hand?" Mick reached for a plate.

Ursula's hand arrived first and his hand rested on her gloved fingers. She retracted her hand and rushed down the hallway.

"She's probably your type anyway," said Mick. "You tend to attract the crazy ones."

"She's just been separated from the outside world too long," said Aiden.

"As soon as the blizzard stops, we should get back out there. On our way here, I saw a large storage shed that might have tents. It's not like anyone's around to care." Mick put on his jacket. "I'll be back soon. Behave while I'm gone." Mick cocked an eyebrow as he left the house.

Aiden wandered down the hallway. On his right, the musty smell wafted from his room. Ursula stood by the bedside table.

"Are you okay?" he asked.

In her glove, she cradled the silver locket. Her eyes gazed to some other place or some other time.

"Is this your mother?" Aiden picked up the photo frame. "You must miss her."

Ursula's dark eyes showed no sign of loss or recollection and she simply laid the locket back on the bedside table.

Aiden waited for her to respond, until it was unbearable. "Can I use your bathroom?"

Without words, Ursula led him across the hall to a cool tiled bathroom.

The musty smell of the bedroom subsided, replaced by something pungent: a mixture reminiscent of part-hospital and part-pub. Dozens of jars cluttered the bathroom windowsill. Inside the jars, animal remains floated in clear fluid: bones, claws and pinkish bits Aiden assumed were organs. Traces of the doc's past research? Aiden turned to Ursula to ask, but she'd already disappeared.

Tiptoeing across the floor, out of fear of knocking anything over, he turned on the taps above the basin and splashed water on his face. Above him, the bathroom cabinet beckoned. Curiosity overcame him and he discovered dozens of used razors. Traces of Dr. Foreston's hair clogged the blades. The old man certainly hadn't shaven recently. Puzzled, he picked up one of the razors and tugged at the fine white hairs in the blades.

A guttural scream interrupted his train of through. Aiden ran to the window and peered outside. Through the falling snow, he saw a glimpse of two polar bears. And Mick was out there with them.

Aiden raced out of the bathroom, down the corridor and out the front door. Cold stabbed him as he looked upon the deserted township. Something growled in the distance. Along the snow-covered street, creamy fur glistened in the light. Long snout, beady eyes and tubby belly — that was how he recalled polar bears. He envisaged them sliding playfully on bellies and pounding ice sheets in search of seals. Occasionally standing on hind legs, but he didn't remember them walking so upright.

"Dr. Foreston," Aiden shouted towards the house. "We need help." Aiden took a cautious few steps down the street. The polar bear mimicked him, walking with surprising agility. And it kept walking. Cold and numbness penetrated Aiden's feet, moved through his legs and into his chest, which froze in an agonising spasm. This was too close for comfort. He rushed back to the house.

He tugged on the door handle. It didn't budge. "Dr. Foreston! Open the door. Ursula!" The bears walked faster. They almost ran.

"Come on, open the door." He rammed it with his shoulder. The handle turned and he fell forward.

Flat on the floor, he panted with icy breath. "Polar bears, two. Huge. And quick."

"Hah! I think you hit your head too hard." Dr Foreston ignored Aiden and walked down the hallway.

"Wait! Mick needs help."

The doctor didn't respond.

Aiden rushed to the phone and called the pilot.

"You need to pick us up now," he screamed down the line when the pilot answered.

"Huh," mumbled the pilot.

Someone knocked on the wooden door. Shit, Mick was still out there.

"Just get here soon." Aiden hung up and raced to the door. He opened it and stared into black beady eyes and a white furry face.

The bear growled.

Aiden screamed.

He staggered backwards and fell near the fireplace. The bear picked up a fire poker, holding it deftly in its paws. He'd only seen polar bears in old documentaries, but he was sure their paws weren't so slender.

He scanned the fireplace for another weapon: an iron pipe, a stick, anything. As the bear loomed down, Aiden grabbed a handful of ash and hurled it at the bear's face.

It howled and pawed at its eyes.

He dodged the beast and ran down the hallway. "Dr. Foreston! Ursula!"

He flung each door open along the corridor, only to be greeted by vacant musty rooms.

He flung open the last door along the corridor and tumbled down a small flight of stairs, hitting his head as he landed. The pungent smell in the room stood out more than the throbbing in his head. Aiden finally recognised the hospital-pub like smell from the bathroom: formaldehyde, which he and Mick used in biology classes. He rubbed his head and gazed around the laboratory.

In the dim light, he spotted benches with Bunsen burners, vials and more specimen jars. Beakers connected to tubes and cylinders spanned the extent of the benches. Aiden's skin tingled.

A dull wooden thud resonated above him. Aiden looked up and saw another staircase leading to an open trapdoor, swinging in the breeze. Something dripped down from the trapdoor onto the floorboards. He touched the sticky liquid. Red liquid. The trail of blood led down the stairs and towards a bench in the far corner of the room. The bench was dotted body parts, vials of blood. And a severed foot with a snow-boot still attached.

Mick?

Aiden's hold on reality began to fray at the edges. Dry-retching, he stumbled backwards into a bench. A cylinder toppled and shattered like crystal confetti on the floor. From the glass wreckage, a foetal being stirred sluggishly before collapsing.

Guttural howling resonated from the doorway as a polar bear

descended the stairs. Aiden raced for the trapdoor and careered into Dr. Foreston.

"What have you done? I think the bears have killed Mick!" A lump grew in his throat, a mixture of anger and grief. "We need to find Ursula. We need to leave. Your crazy breeding program has gone wrong."

"Hah. Polar bears!" Dr. Foreston's arms were suddenly around Aiden neck pressing on his windpipe. "What is the point of breeding more polar bears if they can't adapt? But if they had *our* dexterity combined with *their* strength, they would be invincible. If they are to survive they need to be more brutal, more aggressive, more... human."

"What!" gasped Aiden, tugging at Dr Foreston's arms.

"Do you know how long it takes to get rations of meat here?"

The polar bear growled and staggered forward on hind legs.

Aiden's chest tightened. "You fed... Mick to... them?"

"Don't be absurd. Not all of him."

The creature raised its slender paws above Aiden's head. Aiden scanned the bench for any sign of a weapon. No jars sat in close range, just Mick's foot. He let go of Dr. Foreston's grip around his neck and grasped at the bloody foot.

"Hah! A foot is no use against a thousand pounds of muscular flesh. However, it is very useful for DNA. My babies don't breed. I need fresh DNA specimens. You on the other hand..."

As the creature's claw descended, Aiden rammed the foot into Dr Foreston's groin. Yelping, the doc clutched his groin and released his grip.

Aiden ran for the trapdoor and the bear swiped at Dr Foreston's head instead. The doctor fell to the floor with his neck bent at an acute angle. The creature looked up from the doctor's limp body and growled. Aiden raced through the trapdoor, out onto snow.

As he ran from the scene, his tears solidified in frozen rivulets. He stopped to rest against a giant tundra buggy with mammoth tyres towering over his head. Growling resonated down the road. He hid inside the buggy and had a moment of relief until the handle of the tundra buggy turned. A polar bear stepped inside and walked down the aisle with methodical steps. Aiden raced to the back of the buggy and jimmied open a window. His stomach churned at the long *long* drop below. He shut his eyes, took a breath and jumped.

Aiden's knees crumpled beneath him as he landed in a patch of pink snow. He inspected his limbs for wounds and then realised the blood wasn't his. He looked up and saw Ursula crouched over a lifeless Mick. Her head hung low and white hair flowed across her face concealing her distress. Mick's jacket was shredded, the insulated lining ripped out. Gashes chequered his torso and face. Aiden let out a whimper and placed his hand on Ursula's shoulder.

"It's too late for Mick. The polar bears aren't polar bears. Your dad's mad." He wiped the tears from his cheek and squatted beside her. Ursula's white gloves lay upon Mick's motionless chest. Aiden picked them up.

"Here. We need to go now." Aiden said consolingly and handed her the gloves.

Ursula's hands clasped the gloves, her paws clasped the gloves, her white furry paws clasped the gloves.

Aiden recoiled.

Ursula peered up at him with a mixed look of confusion and empathy. Her mouth was covered in blood. She stared at Aiden helplessly with dark eyes.

"Wha... who..." Aiden staggered backwards. "But... you're human, you're..."

Ursula wiped her mouth with the back of her slender paw, smearing blood across her face. Now pink, he could see her face was covered in a fine white down. They weren't Dr. Foreston's razors.

"The lock of hair — you didn't survive. Ursula didn't survive, did she?"

She seemed to search for some distant memory. The words "Ursula" formed on her slender lips without sound.

"He couldn't save you and your mother, but he had your lock of baby hair. He could bring you back. He could give you strength and swimming ability, enough to survive another tragedy." A cold shiver rippled over Aiden's skin. Growling intensified behind him, but he stood frozen. He should be scared, but she didn't look like the others; she still looked human. "We need to go. It's okay, we'll get you help."

64

Ursula's mouth parted revealing yellowing blood stained teeth and she growled.

Aiden dropped the gloves and fled. He raced down the side streets and alleyways. His feet sank deep into the snow as if he was running through quicksand. Heading for the lake, he ran out onto the ice until there was nothing but dark blue water in front of him.

The lake crooned softly as a light wind wafted onto the land. Behind him, something growled; below him, something creaked. He looked around. A creature wandered from town towards the lake, another approached from the right of the lake and two staggered on their hind legs to his left. Aiden took a step backwards. The ice cracked. He hit water; icy water hit him back, like knives piercing his skin.

Gasping, he breached the surface only to see four white creatures on the shore. A paw swung. He ducked under the water and bobbed up again several feet away. Icy water crept down his jacket collar and down his back, burning his skin. With heavy water-laden clothes, he kept swimming until the creatures were dots on the horizon.

He veered out at a right angle, hoping to hit the shore again. Crystal blue surrounded him: an expansive liquid desert. He looked around. Nothing. Nothing but water.

Fatigued and wheezing, he stopped. His legs and arms felt like lead weights. Aiden's head ducked under the water. A rush of cold seared his brain. He thrashed his arms bringing himself back to the surface and tried to swim further.

He swam endlessly. The blue engulfed him. Above, around and below — nothing but chilly blue. No white. No ice. Nothing solid.

His head ducked under the water and he gasped. Liquid silence.

Then an angelic chopping noise resonated from the skies. In a last-ditch attempt, Aiden thrashed at the water to stay afloat. A ladder fell from a helicopter above. With every ounce of strength that remained, he grasped the ladder and pulled himself up into the helicopter.

He lay panting next to the pilot. "G-g-go now," he said shivering.

The pilot looked around at the white furry creatures surrounding the lake. "Polar bears. Wow. They don't look quite like I imagined."

"Yes, they're slightly different." Aiden sat up and peered out the window.

The pilot hovered above the snow plains. "Wait, there's someone down there... a young lady. Geez, polar bears and girls. You boys did alright."

Aiden spotted Ursula, her face stained with blood.

"She looks injured. We have to help her. The polar bears might hurt her," said the pilot.

Aiden lifted the helicopter pilot's earmuffs and screamed hoarsely, "There are no more polar bears. Go!"

*

From the hillside, she sees the lake has completely thawed. She sniffs the air and walks down the hill away from her den. A ball of fur follows her. And another. The cubs flop onto their bellies and glide down the snowy slope. They toss and turn over one another playfully. As her cubs suckle up to her, she gazes upwards. High in the sky the strange eagle soars, hastily flying south for spring.

The Perisphere Solution
By Robert J. Mendenhall

The frozen terrain that was once Chicago flashed past the flyer's forward canopy in lengthy shadows, a ravaged wasteland of eviscerated buildings and eroded skyscrapers. Jagged spikes of brick and steel jutted at random angles from scabs of glacial ice like so many tombstones. The day-time sky was a perpetual gun-metal gray, sometimes a shade lighter, sometimes darker, but always a thick veil between ground and sun. Nothing moved down there that wasn't blown by arctic wind. Nothing. And somewhere in the frigid fog, beyond the dead city, languished Lake Michigan, its water frozen over for more than three hundred years.

The sight depressed me, as it always did. It depressed me in ways few could imagine, because so few were allowed outside the confines and controlled environments of the city-spheres. Fewer still were permitted to venture this close to urban ruins and see, first-hand, the devastation wrought by a global climate crash—Mother Nature in her fury. As a Federal Agent, I was one of those few.

I banked the flyer in a wide arc until the desolate countryside completely filled my field of vision. The seat-bucket's restraining field secured me against the forces of inertia. I completed my turn and leveled off, heading straight south and away from the ruins.

"Warning. You are approaching restricted air space." The voice that droned from the flyer's control console was androgynous, with a monotone delivery that shouted A.I. "Descend to three thousand feet and pair with North Am City 4-17 Terminal Approach Control."

Relinquishing my control of anything was something I did not do willingly. But, if I ignored the robotic directive, there was a good chance I might be shot down by defense turrets from the city-sphere's prime Trylon. Or I might fly right into a PTB--Power Transmission Beam--and sizzle to a crisp. I found neither scenario appealing.

I descended as instructed and reduced my speed accordingly. A few keystrokes and my flyer's navigation logic paired with Terminal Approach Control. I lifted my hands mockingly, as if something magical had happened rather than something digital, and sat back in my padded pilot bucket. I felt the flyer nudge slightly as the TAC air traffic logic adjusted my course, and I frowned at the implied criticism of my navigational skills.

The scarred ground continued to race past me, mile after mile of frigid misery.

North Am 4-17 was the official, sterile designation assigned to the spherical city by the Council on Climate Survival of the Unified Nations. It accurately reflected the city's continental location, regional position on that continent, and UN charter sequence. Unofficially, we simply called it Peoria.

As the flyer slowed on final approach, the sight ahead renewed me. As it always did. I felt the despondency within me decant away, and I smiled in appreciation at the contrast between the cadaverous landscape and the geometrically perfect, artificial structures which defied nature, declaring with certainty that man would not be subjugated by it.

The city-sphere stood a full mile in diameter, perfectly round and shimmering with an opalescent aqua-marine that seemed to soothe the wounded ground surrounding it. It appeared to hover above the surface, but this was an illusion of perspective. In reality, a series of support pylons, each an eighth of a mile in diameter and a quarter-mile high nestled the sphere at its base.

The flyer banked around the first of three prime Trylons surrounding the sphere like watch towers. A slim, three-sided needle, two miles high from squat base to narrow peak, each Trylon radiated the same, warm glow as the sphere it overlooked.

The flyer descended another two thousand feet and slowed to just over stall speed.

"Identity confirmed," the voice droned. "Welcome to North Am City 4-17, Special Agent Markon. You have been granted priority clearance to the city. Your aircraft will be parked in the Federal garage located on Mezzanine Level Three. Upon arrival, please proceed—"

The instructions were cut off by a high-pitched whoop-whoop, and a toneless, metallic voice.

"Alert. Security breach, Outpost SS417."

Son of a bitch, that was fast. Would it be that easy?

I decoupled from Terminal Approach Control even as the coordinates were coming in. I didn't wait for the sequence to complete; I knew where I was going. I banked, barrel-rolled, and cranked the flyer's throttle wide open.

"Nature of breach," I asked.

"Outer entry hatch accessed with decoy code. Inner hatch not yet accessed."

I sped away from the sphere less than one hundred feet above the surface ice.

"Correction," the mechanical voice said. "Inner hatch accessed,"

Another voice reverberated through the cockpit. This one human, female, and far from toneless.

"Markon, what the hell are you—"

I cut the transmission and dropped another fifty feet, well below the sphere's sensor deck.

"Nearest back-up unit?" I asked the mechanical voice.

"There are no Federal units on station."

Not that I expected any. We were spread very thin across the North American continent.

"Scan the immediate area of the outpost for vehicles or life signs," I instructed.

"Scan completed. No vehicles or life signs detected."

I didn't like that. "Scan the interior of the outpost for life signs."

"Unable to scan the interior of the outpost."

Shit. I forgot this outpost was shielded.

"Display relief map of the area."

A holographic chart of the area in relief grid materialized in front of me. A solid shape stood out within one of the undulations of line-- the outer hatch. I pinpointed a rise about a mile from the hatch and steered wide around the area heading toward that spot. I slowed and came in silent. The flyer settled behind the small peak with barely a puff of disturbed snow. I shut the flyer down and locked the controls

The temperature outside was negative 38 degrees centigrade. Practically balmy for this time of year. I inched out of my bucket and reached behind it for a snow suit. The cockpit was cramped and it took me precious minutes to squirm into the one-piece environmental jumpsuit. I had to remove my cape in order to get a tight seal. I pulled the hood over my head and adjusted the face plate, then toggled the suit on. Warm air hissed, slightly inflating the suit.

I popped open the canopy.

After climbing down to the ground, I secured the canopy and pulled a personal jet pack from the aircraft's storage boot. A moment later, I flittered toward the outpost about a dozen feet off the surface at 20 miles an hour, the top speed of the pack's magnetic drive unit. My snow suit's gray and white color rendered me practically invisible against the glacial ice.

Minutes later, I was outside the outpost exterior door, my back flat against the ice, sonic pistol snuggled tightly in my gloved hands. The speakers in my hood relayed the whisper of wind around me, but no other sounds. There were no other flyers or ground vehicles to be seen. No tracks or footprints in the veil of snow cover other than my own.

I surmised there were two possibilities. The first was whoever used the decoy access codes we leaked had used a jet pack similar to my own to hover over the ground while they keyed in the codes or...

The decoy codes were transmitted remotely.

Shit.

If scenario number two was true, this was likely a test of the leaked access codes. To see what would happen if they were used. And I just showed them exactly what would happen.

I looked around for a camera drone, or something that would suggest surveillance. Nothing I could see.

Shit. Shit. Shit.

I keyed in the decoy codes and the exterior hatch popped open. It took less than two minutes for me to ascertain that no one was inside and that nothing had been damaged or stolen. Ten minutes later, pissed at myself, I was back in my flyer and speeding back toward Peoria.

"Warning," The androgynous voice told me for the second time. "You are approaching restricted air space. Descend to three thousand feet and pair with—"

A series of short tones interrupted the canned monologue, followed by a brief burst of light from on the canopy's heads-up display. A holographic head coalesced in the air between me and the display, slightly translucent but extremely detailed. And huge. The head was easily five times the size of the sender's. A woman's head, it hovered slightly above me, glaring down on me as if to make it clear who was really in charge here.

The thick headband that encircled her forehead was scarlet; my own headband was jet black. Her thick, amber hair was tucked under the headband and seemed to glitter, but I knew this was the effect of the transmission, and not its true nature. The sparkle in her cyan eyes, I knew from experience, was genuine. So was the scowl of her salmon lips. Unconsciously, my eyes drifted to those lips. One could not help it. They were full and rounded, and right now nearly filled my vision. They seemed moist, but this, too, was a holographic effect. Reluctantly, I shifted my gaze to the arch of her jaw line, the shadows of her throat, and to the golden rank pins on her stiff, scarlet collar. As if they had independent wills of their own, my eyes dropped beneath her collar, scanning the empty air below for more of her.

"Eyes on mine, Markon." Her voice boomed too loudly in the enclosed space of the flyer's cockpit. I grimaced.

"Tone it down, Tam. I'm right here," I said.

I swear I saw those oversized lips twitch into a brief smirk. I must have imagined it, though. Captain Tamar Getty rarely smiled.

"This better?" she asked. At a normal decibel level, her voice was a pleasant sound, a bit husky without losing any femininity. In fact, the slight roughness of it accentuated her allure.

And I certainly "allured" her.

"Much better. But, why the call?" I asked.

"What the hell are you up to?"

I opened my mouth to answer. I didn't have a chance.

"Why did you break off from TAC?" she demanded.

I opened my mouth to answer, but…

"Where did you fly off to?"

I opened my mouth…

"What are you doing in my jurisdiction?"

"Relax, Tam—" I managed to get in.

"Captain Getty," she corrected.

"Relax, Captain," I elongated her rank in a way I knew annoyed her. "I was going to contact you as soon as I made it through the Entry Control Point."

"You should have done that before—"

Now I was getting annoyed. "Stow it, Tam. You'll understand when we meet. Your office. One hour."

I made sure she saw me drop my gaze to her holographic lips before I waved the transmission closed.

I settled back in my bucket and let TAC guide my flyer in to the sphere's transportation center. I passed underneath the sphere and traveled nearly a half mile to a wide, cylindrical structure protruding from the bottom of the sphere at its midpoint. The flyer hovered several hundred feet from the Terminal arrival gate as a passenger shuttle drifted inside. A moment later, my craft slid forward and through the same gate.

I fidgeted impatiently in my seat as my flyer was scanned, registered, and finally tethered to a holding berth in the reception garage. I shut the systems down and popped open the canopy. A ground crew robot, gleaming in a silver and electric-blue body casing, flew a saucer-shaped hover-sled up to my open cockpit.

"Welcome to North Am City 4-17, Citizen," the robot metallically toned. "Do you have luggage?"

"I do not," I responded crisply as I stepped into the open sled. It gave just a bit, but righted itself as it adjusted to my presence. I gathered the folds of my ebony cape and sat on the cushioned bench that circled the sled's interior. Immediately, I felt the soft pressure of a restraining field encircle my torso.

"Does your conveyance require service or fueling?" the robot asked.

"Both," I said.

"Understood, sir. I have scheduled the necessary maintenance automatons."

"Thank you. It'll be parked in the Federal garage."

"Noted, sir."

The sled dipped and angled toward the Terminal Entry Control Point. Similar sleds, all flown by robot greeters, whizzed around the garage, high and low, forward and back, left and right. The sleds made soft chirping noises that grew in pitch and cadence the faster they went. Not that they could go very fast in the reception garage. Still, the overall effect was almost musical. The robot in my sled was clean and polished, but I could smell old lubricant from its joints and heard the coarse whir of its timeworn servo-mechanisms.

The greeter dropped me at the Entry Control Point, bid me a great day, and chirped back into the reception garage to ferry more arrivals. I showed my credentials to the security officer at the ECP and was directed to a short line at the far end. I ignored the glares of the new arrivals I just by-passed, who had to go through the full-spectrum security sweep. As a Federal agent I had a lot of leeway and a few privileges. This was one of them.

Thirty minutes later I was through ECP and riding a carousel car up through the Terminal levels to the atrium level. I stepped out of the crowded car and into the opulent, open air of Peoria. The ground beneath my leather boots was soft and earthy, thick with grass that was lush and as green as it could be. A slight breeze warmed my face. I unfastened my cape and pulled it from my shoulders. A blue jay flapped ferociously above me, followed by several more in playful pursuit. I heard gentle wind chimes nearby and took in a pleasing scent that might have followed a spring shower in the ancient past. As I often did when I transitioned from outside to in-sphere, I closed my eyes and raised my chin, savoring the feeling. Relishing the contrast.

After a moment, I opened my eyes and gazed upward into the cylindrical space that stretched nearly a mile straight up through one hundred terraces to the very top of the sphere. We called this great, central expanse "the courtyard." A quarter-mile in diameter, it teemed with clouds and birds and the whisper of wind. Occasionally, you'd see a man or woman slowly gliding in personal hover packs, capes rippling behind them. Each terrace encircled the courtyard like open balconies, following the entire circumference of the sphere. A wide, spiraling ramp connected one terrace to the next, corkscrewing all the way up to Terrace 1. With its oxygen-replenishing landscaping, the winding ramp was a popular venue for casual walker, hikers, and runners.

I teetered as a pair of toga-clad children playing a game of tag nearly knocked me over. A small dog yipped after them. Giddy music played from a nearby bistro. Couples strolled hand-in hand, headband to headband, laughing. Loving. It was idyllic. It was like a golden age had come upon humanity.

My elation petered away when I recalled why I was here and what was at stake. And what was to come.

Sobered, I crossed the open park to the bank of express tubes at the far end of the atrium. I selected an empty tube and stepped onto the platform.

"Equatorville ," I instructed the tube.

"Unable to determine destination," the tube announced in the same gender-neutral voice that Terminal Approach Control used.

Of course not.

"Terrace 50," I said.

"Terrace 50 confirmed," the tube said.

I felt the same pressure around my body that signaled an activated motion suppression field, and a moment later I sped upward through the tube at 250 feet per second. It took less than ten seconds to reach Terrace 50 and I hardly felt the motion. The field released me when the platform reached my destination. I stepped onto the Central Services Terrace, colloquially referred to as Equatorville, because it was midway up the sphere at roughly the equatorial plane.

Again, I swooned at the engineering marvel of the city. Because of its spheroid shape, as you rose from the equator, each terrace was geometrically smaller than the one below it. Conversely, as you descended from the equator, each terrace was geometrically smaller than the one *above* it. The highest and lowest terraces were mainly support and operations-oriented, while those more central were residential and recreational. Whenever I tried to compute the volume of each level based on the radius and circumference at a given point in the sphere and the number of people that could comfortably live in a spherical city, factoring in heat displacement and air movement in a closed environment, ceiling height based on open space ratios... I usually wound up with a migraine.

I made my way along the main boulevard to the Public Safety Headquarters Building. The streets were teeming with people walking or riding on the terrace tram. Though there was little wind, capes flowed from motion. I still carried mine. There was a subtle scent of mint on this level, probably introduced at the ventilator to instill a sense of cleanliness. It worked.

I stepped through the open arch of the Public Safety Headquarters Building and into the entry foyer. A golden robot, slightly taller than me and quite a bit bulkier, stood as the solitary piece of furniture in the room. Both arms displayed a glossy blue hologram of the public safety logo. A silver shield twinkled holographically on the robot's left pectoral plate.

I approached.

"Greetings, Citizen." That same, asexual tone emanated from a speaker grill where a human mouth would have been on a real person. "How may I direct you?"

"Greetings, Robot," I mocked it to no avail. "I am Federal Agent Redg Markon here to see Captain Getty."

"Do you have an appointment?"

"I do not; however, she is expecting me."

"One moment, please." The robot did not move or blink or whir in any way. I watched it intently, but it didn't alter its implacable visage. I suspected the optical nodes were cameras, so I shuffled as close as I could to the metal appliance and leaned into it, tilting my head so my left eye was peering into the robot's left node. The optical node flashed and I staggered back blinking.

"Son of a bitch..." I muttered. I swear the machine chuckled.

"Captain Getty will see you," the robot drolled. "Her office is located—"

"I know where it is, Flashbulb."

I side-stepped the robot, rubbing my eye.

Tamar's office was mid-way down the hall and about as close to the Chief of Public Safety's office as you could get without being his secretary. I strolled through the portal and smiled at her receptionist, a middle-aged officer with a silver headband and nothing on his navy-blue collar.

"Agent Markon. Good to see you again," he said pleasantly.

"Good to see you too, Officer Janos. She in?"

He nodded. "And in a foul mood."

"So, all is normal."

"It got worse when she found out you were in the jurisdiction."

I smiled again. "What can I say?"

"Go on in," Janos said.

Tamar's office was larger than the reception area, but not by much. An oval work station faced the door and it was littered with holographic projections. The walls were tastefully adorned with motion sculptures in a variety of colors. The one I saw first was a burgundy and brown representation of an extinct horse in full gallop. The office was dimly lit. In fact, most of the illumination came from the large window that let in the aqua-marine light radiating from the sphere's inner hull.

Tamar Getty swiped at a hologram and it blinked out. She stood, fists on hips, and eyed me with disdain. I felt the tug of attraction that always occurred when I first saw her after a prolonged absence. It had been nearly a year this time.

She was cape-less at the moment; it hung on a cape rack in the corner. I always said her scarlet and gold uniform should never be concealed by a cape. Looking at her now, the way her uniform hugged her frame and accentuated her form, I would say it again.

"How's the eye?" she quipped.

I blinked. "Funny. Did you flash me yourself? Or did you have your lackey do it for you?"

"Oh, I pulled the trigger myself. Now what the hell are you doing in my city?"

"Oh, I hadn't realized you had been appointed City Manager. When did that happen?"

She clenched her jaw. "What. Are. You. Doing. Here." She spaced out each word with exaggerated articulation. Her normally light complexion had reddened to nearly the same shade of scarlet as her headband. And with her full amber hair, it looked as if her head was aflame. I decided to forgo my normally charming aloofness and got down to business.

"Relax, Captain." I sat in the guest chair in front of her desk. She dropped back into her seat behind the desk and waved the holo-images away. Her color began to return. I peered over my shoulder at the open portal. "Do you mind?"

She said nothing, but waved her hand over a small orb inlaid in the desktop and the portal to the reception area shimmered closed. "We're secure," she said.

I wasted no time. "Last week there was an incident of sorts at 61."

"I didn't see anything from North-Am. Are you sure?"

"I was there, Tam. North-Am locked it down right away."

"What's the story?" She leaned forward, hands folded on her desk. She was interested. That was good.

"It occurred at one of North-Am 61's outlying industrial compounds. One of the sub-Trylons was deliberately taken off-line, interrupting the PTB to the compound. Fortunately, this was an automated facility so the only thing that froze was the machinery. No permanent damage. North-Am claimed jurisdiction because the compound that was taken offline was a Federal facility."

She sat up straight and thrust her face forward. Here it comes.

"A Federal facility? What the hell is the North American Command doing with a Federal facility on municipal ice?"

"It was just a small post, Tam."

"Small post? Surveillance post, maybe? An eavesdropper? Were the Feds monitoring the sphere? Violating Citizen Rights? Again?"

"It's not like that," I tried to explain.

She stood and paced, never taking her eyes off my face. I felt my forehead itch beneath my headband.

"Really, Markon? Really? Then tell me, what is it like? What were the Feds doing there, and why are you here? Is there a…"

I looked away.

"Son of a bitch," she spat. "You have an eavesdropper here at 47, don't you? At one of the outliers. Don't you."

I said nothing.

"Answer me, damn it!"

I stood and approached her. "Yes, we have a Federal facility here. But it is not a surveillance station."

"What is it?"

"I can't tell you. It's classified."

"Classified?" She got very close to me, well into my personal space.

77

Normally, I would have relished her proximity, but this wasn't intimacy. It was hostility. I stepped back. She stepped forward. "Classified? But not an eavesdropper?"

"It's not the way you think."

"I think it is exactly the way I think."

"Okay," I said. "I get it. You're a cop and you're suspicious. I respect that, but Tamar, you have an irrational distrust of the Federal government. We're your—"

"If you say the government is my friend, so help me I will hit you so fucking hard you'll wake up in Equaterville Medical Center next week. Or the week after."

That wasn't quite what I was going to say, but it was close enough so I changed tracks. "Look, you're forgetting it was the Federal government that stepped up when the ice came and billions of people in the United States and Canada were killed. It was the Federal government that fast-tracked the Perisphere Solution that saved nearly as many as had been lost. Every government on the planet has since built spheres and it was the Fed—"

"Enough." She pivoted away shaking her head. "I don't need a history lesson. What the hell are you doing here?"

"Okay. Yes, we have a Federal facility on North-Am 47's ice. No, it is not an eavesdropper, and yes, we believe it is a target."

"Who's targeting it?"

"I can't..." I let it trail away.

"I know." She fingered air quotes of her own. "It's classified."

I remained silent.

She sat and looked at me. Her unyielding face yielded just a bit. "You know," she said finally. "The entire time we were married, I couldn't shut you up. Now, when I want you to talk to me, you won't. How messed up is that?"

"Messed up," I agreed.

"Redg," she said softly. "I want to help you. If you tell me this site of yours is legit, then I will believe you. But, I can't go into the Chief's office and tell him that his City Security Commander is investigating something of which she knows nothing, that occurred at a location she's not aware of, involving suspects she hasn't a clue about. He'll think we're off getting laid."

I smiled. "Not one to lead a fellow law enforcement professional astray, I say we do just that." I thought I might have pushed it beyond the limit with that remark. I expected her to explode. Instead, she let slip a stiff smile.

But she did not concur.

"How about if I make a call to my boss at North-Am One and have her reach out to your Chief?" I offered.

She thought about that for a moment. "He's still going to think we're off getting laid."

I nodded and pulled my phone-pad from my belt. One could only hope, I thought.

*

Properly cleared by her Chief, Tamar and I rode a tube down to the atrium and then a carousel car down to the Terminal. We requisitioned an off-schedule bullet car and, in relatively no time at all, we were rocketing through the transparent tube atop the arched tramway toward prime Trylon Alpha, three miles from the sphere. It took only minutes to traverse the distance.

The Trylon Security Commander met us at the Debarkation Point at the base of the Trylon.

"Captain Getty," Lieutenant Rik Tanis extended his hand as Tamar and I stepped onto the passenger platform. Tanis was an older officer, dark-skinned with curly black hair creased with gray and trimmed close to his scalp. He wore a white headband and cape.

"Rik," she said and pumped his offered hand. "Thanks for meeting us."

"No need to thank me," he explained. "The Chief assigned me to assist you. What do you need?"

"Let's head to your office," I said, interjecting myself into their conversation.

Tanis looked at me, then shot a questioning glance at Tamar.

"It's okay, Rik. He's a Fed."

Tanis blew out a breath that was blatantly not a gesture of approval. I followed behind them at a "safe" distance.

I had been in prime Trylons before, so I was not impressed by the sheer immensity of it. A communications array at the tip 2 miles up, defensive gun turrets on all three sides at 1.5 miles and a power transmission node at 1 mile dedicated and paired to the sphere. The Trylon was positioned far enough away so that if some catastrophe caused it to topple, it wouldn't crash into the sphere. This Trylon was dedicated to agricultural support of the sphere. Between the crops and livestock, there was a unique grassy-manure odor in the air that not even the scrubbers could eliminate. It screamed farm.

We rode the central tube to the midpoint, where the Trylon Public Safety Annex maintained its offices. As we rose, I looked out at level after level of farmland, all tended by robots and automatons. I was heavy with an internal conflict— pride in what we had accomplished as a society since the climate crash, and remorse, maybe even fear, for what I knew was to come. I glanced at Tamar and saw that she was staring at me. She raised an eyebrow, our silent shorthand for *What's bothering you?* I pouted my bottom lip, meaning: *We'll talk later.* She flared her nostrils, and I smiled at the insult.

Tanis' office was no bigger than Tamar's, but tightly crammed with equipment, monitors, and a huge desk laden with holographs. There were two seats, the one behind the desk and the one in front of it. Tanis dropped into his. Tamar stepped back, so I sat in the other.

I wasted no time. I briefed Tanis on the incident at the North-Am 61 and the direction my investigation had taken. I left out classified details, such as what the facility was, and the nature of its mission. He didn't press me on it.

"Okay," Tanis said. "So why are you here?"

"We made an arrest. The suspect subsequently gave up a number of his co-conspirators. One of them is here."

"In Peoria," Tanis said.

"Specifically, here in this Trylon."

"What's his name?"

"Her name. Miri Anton. She's a power distribution technician. I would like to question her."

Tanis shot a glance to Tamar. She remained outwardly impassive, but I knew her. I knew she had reacted to what I had said. It was like the air around her had been disturbed. Tanis had probably not caught it. But I did.

"A Federal agent wants to question a city citizen," Tanis said. His eyes, his tone, his clenched fist, all displayed his distaste. "Do you have a warrant?"

I had been through this before. It was the norm to be suspicious of the Federal government. No one remembered the good we did. That we still do. They only remembered the unpopular decisions that affected their lives.

"I don't have a warrant. I have a request. If Anton does not want to talk to me, that will be that. I'll leave quietly and without incident. At that point; however, I will fly to North-Am One and get that warrant. I will return with it and I will arrest her. Then I'll ask my questions. Lieutenant Tanis. Look, I applaud your commitment to your citizen's rights and best interests. It tells me you're a good cop. But, I have a job to do and I'm looking out for North-Am's best interests which, whether you believe it or not, include every citizen in the nation. And that's what makes me a good Federal agent."

"Nice speech. Agent." Clearly I had not won him over. "But, I've heard that best for the nation crap before."

Before I could respond, Tamar did. "Rik, we just want to talk to her. If she's involved in something that could endanger the city, we should at least try to learn what that is."

Tanis pulled off his headband, methodically smoothed the material, and repositioned it over his forehead. It was all very dramatic. He finally looked up at me with eyes of ice.

"All she has to say is no, and we're done," he said

"Agreed," I said.

We spent the next several minutes looking at Miri Anton's public record and work history. Nothing stood out that would implicate her in a plot to overthrow the government, or even inconvenience it. We took the tube down to the ground level Power Distribution Center. This was the control point for the sub-Trylon transmitters that broadcast power to their receiver-mates in the outlying industrial compounds. She was easy to find. Most labor in the Trylon was accomplished by golden-cased robots. She was the only human there.

Miri Anton was not petite. She was easily my height, though soft in her arms and hefty in her middle. She wore her hair bobbed short and, despite social convention, did not wear a headband. Her face was oval and flat, her skin pock-marked. She wore wrinkled overalls stained with I knew not what.

She looked up from her console at our approach. If she recognized any of us, she didn't say so.

"Can I help you?" she asked. "This is a restricted area."

Tanis casually moved his snow-white cape to the side to display his badge. "Miri Anton?" he asked.

In response, she kicked over her stool and ran like that extinct steed on Tamar's wall.

Each side of the prime Trylon's triangular base was a quarter mile in length. There wasn't a whole lot of distance she could put between us, but there was a great deal of machinery and conduits she could hide behind. Tamar pursued Anton directly. Tanis cut to the left, I cut to the right.

A shot rang out. I dove for the nearest rack and drew my sonic pistol even before I had completed my roll. I thumbed the charging switch and the pistol hummed.

Another shot. Actually, three shots so close together they sounded like one. Tamar. She had the quickest trigger finger I'd ever seen. The first sonic pulse barely had time to impact before she let lose another and then another.

We had to be careful where we pointed our sonic pistols. Even though they fired pulses of solid sound incapable of penetrating a human body, a volley of solid sound could knock a man down, bruise muscle, even break bone. A shot to the eye would do some serious internal damage. We all shot low. Anton, however, did not. Tanis took a round on his forehead. The impact knocked him to the ground and peeled off his headband.

"Miri," I called out in a lull. "We just want to talk to talk—"

Six shots above my head shut me up and drove me down.

I caught sight of Tamar crouched behind some odd apparatus. She signaled me with a curt nod of her head and a wave of her pistol in Anton's general direction. I picked up the shorthand. She wanted me to draw Anton's fire. No problem.

82

I found a shadow nearby and dove for it. My cape trailed behind me and drew Anton's fire. The material rippled with each of her shots. Several pulses impacted my legs.

Son of a bitch, that hurt.

I looked back at Tamar's position, hoping for a concerned glance, but she had already used my distraction to move.

"Miri," I tried again. "You don't need to do this. Let's talk."

"No talk," she shouted back. "You're a Fed. We know what you're up to. All of you. North-Am. The Unified Nations. It won't work, this time. You hear me? We won't be fooled again. We'll expose you! We'll ex—"

No sounds of a scuffle. No whine of a shot. Just silence.

I eased myself from my concealment, sonic gun outstretched. I limped slightly.

"Clear," Tamar said from somewhere ahead.

I angled around a console and saw Tamar standing over the unmoving body of Miri Anton. A lock of Tamar's hair had freed itself from her headband and hung errantly over her forehead. She flipped her golden cape over her shoulder and holstered her pistol.

"Check on Rik, will you?" she asked.

I hobbled over to the unconscious lieutenant. He was breathing.

"He's out cold," I said. "You okay?"

"Yeah," she said. "What was all that crap about her knowing what you were up to and it won't work this time and they won't be fooled again? What's going on, Redg?"

Shit.

"I can't tell you, Tam. It's classified."

She glared at me, as she had done earlier in the day at her office. "You're a prick. You know that, Markon? A first-class—"

I caught sight of a sudden movement to my right and flinched just as a golden worker robot backhanded me across the side of my head. As I went down, I saw the same machine forward-slap Tamar. She fell in a slow-motion swirl, her cape wrapping around her torso, a ribbon of blood trailing from a gash in her face.

My vision doubled and blurred. I tried to push myself up as the robot scooped Tamar, tossed her over its shoulder with no effort, and lumbered toward the exterior hatch. I waddled upright and saw Anton a few feet away from me. I pulled my pistol from my holster with a shaky hand, and started toward her.

Anton held a small pad in her hand. She pressed a membrane on it. The exterior door swung open with a whoosh. Deadly, sub-centigrade air funneled into the Trylon. The robot continued through the open hatch, Tamar still in its clutch.

"Me or her, G-man," Anton shouted over the wind. "You can't have us both."

She turned and darted toward the tube.

I turned and sort of darted toward the hatch.

The air was arctic and hit me so hard I nearly lost consciousness. I cried out as my lung tissue frosted and my eyes began to crystalize. I sank to one knee in the snow. My mind went numb.

A random thought… that by some mathematical quirk, minus 40 degrees Fahrenheit was also minus 40 degrees centigrade. How messed up was that?

I snapped back to pseudo-reality. A few yards ahead I saw the blurry image of the golden robot as it lumbered forward, unhindered by nature. Tamar's cape dangled from her shoulders, and brushed a slight track in the snow as the robot moved.

I refocused. I struggled forward through the bite of the wind and gained on the slow-moving robot. I stepped around it. It turned its head in my direction without breaking stride.

I lifted my pistol, stuck it up against the robot's left ocular node and pulled the trigger.

Again.

And again.

*

Tamar's groan signaled she was waking. I pushed myself, with considerable effort and discomfort, out of the lounge chair and tottered over to her bed. Medical sensors tracked her biometrics and indicated she was stable and improving. And now, she was coming out of her induced coma.

Her eyes fluttered but remained closed. The medical team had removed her headband when she was admitted and this was the first time in a long time I had actually seen her smooth forehead. It was almost like looking at her naked. I feathered my fingertips over her forehead, then the back of my hand over her cheek. She slipped her own hand over mine, surprising me. Her eyes remained closed, but her lips parted and she took a shallow breath.

I closed my fingers around her hand and squeezed just enough to acknowledge her.

"Hey," I whispered.

She opened her eyes. "H-hey," she managed.

"How are you feeling?"

She giggled. "High."

I nodded and smiled. She was pumped up on a load of pain killers and metabolizers. "Been there."

"I'm told you went out after me," she said. Each word was a slow, drawn out effort.

"Yeah, well..." It was one of those very rare occasions when I didn't have a wise-ass remark to make.

"The C-Chief thinks you did it to get laid."

"Well, not one to lead a fellow law enforcement professional astray, you know..."

She giggled, then sobered. "What's going on, Redg?"

I glanced at the portal and saw it was secured. I faced her, thought a moment, and decided.

"Tam, we have Federal facilities at every sphere in North-Am. All the Unified Nations have similar facilities in their zones."

She said nothing, but I knew I had her complete attention.

"They're not surveillance stations. They're seismic stations."

I was committed now. Classified or not, I was bringing her in on the most sensitive intelligence on the planet.

I told her everything. About how climatologists had predicted the climate crash centuries ago, but were ignored until it was too late.

How the Perisphere Solution was designed not only to save humanity from that catastrophe, but from the one yet to come.

How those same climatologists and the geologists that followed, all measured the shift in glacial mass and its effect on the planet's rotation.

How computer model after computer model, decade after decade, forecasted the same, inescapable outcome.

We were going to experience a sudden, violent shifting of the Earth's poles. The planet was going to capsize.

I don't know how long we just looked at each other without speaking. It might have been a minute. Might have been five.

"When?" Tamar finally asked.

"We don't know. The models are inconclusive on that point. It could be a hundred years from now. Could be tomorrow. Hence the seismic stations."

"How long have you been living with this, Redg?"

"A long time, Tam. A long time.

She nodded. "And Anton?"

"She belongs to a radical group going by the name Circular Reasoning."

"What's the significance of that?"

"We have no idea. But they're conspiracy theorists. They don't believe the climate crash actually occurred. They think it's a government hoax, that we made it up to deceive the people. And, by gods, they're going to prove it."

"Are they insane?" Tamar said. "All they have to do is look outside."

"Tam, they don't believe we put a sphere on the moon, either."

She closed her eyes and I could tell she was fading. I caressed her hand.

"Sleep, love."

"Uh huh," she slurred. "Will you... will you be here when I wake up."

"Of course."

I wrapped my cape around my shoulders and walked over to the window. Equatorville Medical Center overlooked the courtyard. From here, I could see across the distance to the far side of the terrace a quarter-mile away. If I craned my neck I could see up nearly all the way to underside of the Operations Level above Terrace 1 nearly half-a-mile up, or all the way down to the green of the atrium park almost half-a-mile below. I saw birds and clouds and the occasional hover-packing person.

And I marveled at the Perisphere Solution, how a concept borrowed from an ancient world's fair attraction had saved the human race from near extinction.

The critical question... would it save us, again?

Kia Manawanui
By Tyree Campbell

She gazed out at Lake Rotomahana as if for the last time. Each year for the past decade she had spent two weeks here in the national park on New Zealand's North Island, staying at the lakeshore cottage left to her by an uncle with the understanding that she would see to its upkeep. There was nothing specific to prevent her from returning next year, should she choose to do so. But the state of the planet was in flux.

Here, in her real life, she was Victoria Elizabeth Chambers, a distant relative of one of the explorers of New Zealand's South Island. Named for two queens of England, she invited a very few to call her Vickie, and several others to shorten the full name to Victoria. In her bill-paying life in the United States, where she worked as an environmental specialist for Ecotect, her colleagues opted for Kiwi, which she loathed, but which had stuck to her like a lamprey to a trout. But the bill-paying life was illusory at best; she was not working to pay the bills, which in any case were few. She was working to save the planet. Worse, she was working to save it from itself. And it did not want to be saved.

Or so it seemed.

Cries filled the morning air; somewhere nearby, a flock of birds had taken off. Some fifty meters away, on the lake, a black swan glided by, haughty and graceful. Victoria sighed softly. Oh, she could stay here, here among the great conifers, like the totara trees with their paperlike flaking bark and the hard wood that the Maori used for their finest carvings. Catch rainbow trout stocked in many of the country's lakes. Breathe fresh air. Water in streams so clear you can count the smooth dark rocks on the bed. It never got old.

What, thought Victoria, *have we done?*

Vegetation clutched at her hiking shoes. She liberated them, wondering whether she was freeing the plants or herself. It was not an idle question. Independence might coexist with interdependence, provided there was respect on both sides. The plants meant her no harm, and vice versa. But.

Again she sighed. But.

In the very moment of her indecision, to stay or to return, she heard something heavy crash through the wild shrubs several meters off to her left. Fear gripped her momentarily; New Zealand had few indigenous fauna of a size to be worrisome, but some dogs had gone wild. Presently she saw it, and stared. A kakapo? How was that possible?

Vast numbers of the ponderous, flightless parrot had been whittled down to a hundred or so, all in protected sanctuaries. This one, clearly, lived in the wild. It seemed to have no fear of her. The size of a small turkey, it lumbered up to her as if to greet her, its beak worrying at a nut. Victoria did not move. The kakapo paused before her for a few seconds, as if debating whether to share its prize. Then it continued on, to vanish into the thick forest west of her cottage.

She took the clumsy bird as a sign. If the kakapo could survive the predations of humanity, then so might humanity itself. She had to go back. But as a species, the kakapo, despite perhaps a few still living in the wild, remained on the verge of extinction. Should she therefore stay?

With a little cry of anguish Victoria tugged at her short yellow hair until her scalp ached. Deep inside, she knew what her decision had to be.

It had to be, one more time. Like Hamlet, she had to take up arms against a sea of troubles.

"*Haere ahau ano,*" she muttered in Maori. I go. She went back inside the cottage to finish packing.

*

From LAX Victoria caught a flight to Albuquerque. Her original plan called for her to go directly to the new main office in Denver, but Michael had texted her to divert, so that she might give a presentation to an elementary school class—and collect donations. She'd protested, but it was difficult to shout when texting, which may have been why he had eschewed Skype on this occasion. When she had balked, excusing herself on the basis of travel-weariness after her long flight across the Pacific, he'd sent a final text, *C'mon, Kiwi, this what U do, rt?* and closed the communication before she'd had a chance to respond.

Kiwi, which she loathed. But he was never, ever Mike. Always Michael.

She rented a car and drove from the airport to Selena Quintanilla Elementary School on the eastern outskirts of the city, parked outside the gate, endured a metal detector scan by the gate guard and an inspection of the plain cardpaper box she was carrying, and followed his instructions to the front office. There once again she was subjected to a metal scan, this one sensitive enough to detect the nail clippers in the overnight travel bag that doubled as her purse. It detected nothing inside the box, however. Under escort to Miss Yolanda's classroom, she found herself wondering just how much time was left each day for education. She wondered whether anyone had caught the irony of the teacher's name being the same as that of the woman who had murdered the school's namesake. But Yolanda was a common enough name in New Mexico, and elsewhere.

Michael, however, was even more common. Half a foot shorter than her six-two, and sixty pounds heavier than her one-fifty-five, and with his black hair vanishing in male-pattern baldness, Michael Terrence Aspen, pudgy and pale, might have been any of several million American men. But only one of them was the president of Ecotect, the organization founded by him to combat abuses to the environment and to reverse by whatever means necessary the various processes by which the Earth's air, water, and land were being polluted. And to receive federal and state grants to do so. Uncommon he was, but common all the same.

Victoria regarded herself as working for Ecotect; Michael regarded her as working for him. Thus, his shameless promotion of her in order to encourage donations. Seven years ago, she had been a reserve on New Zealand's Olympic basketball team. The team had lost all three games in Group E, and she had played but a handful of minutes and scored just nine points, but that didn't matter. Her cachet as Olympic athlete opened contributor doors to her—and to Ecotect. No donation too large, no donation too small—even from elementary school children. The work of Ecotect, after all, had to be financed from many sources.

Once inside the classroom, Victoria recognized the expressions on the faces of the fourth-graders—a mix of excitement and reservation at meeting someone new. Because the best approach was to relate the students to something familiar to them, she had done some meteorological homework. Accordingly, following Miss Yolanda's introduction, she set the cardpaper box down on the teacher's desk and went right to work.

"I heard you had quite a snowstorm about a month ago," she began. "Something like one meter—excuse me, about three feet—of snow in one day."

She saw in their faces that they remembered quite well.

"And you didn't have to go to school for what, three or four days?" she went on. "Is that right?"

Several enthusiastic nods encouraged her, as did a few claims of "Four days."

"And you've never had such a snowstorm before," said Victoria, and glanced at Miss Yolanda. "Is that right?"

Miss Yolanda beamed a smile, and her nut-brown face glowed from its frame of black hair. "I've lived here for almost twenty years," she replied. "This was the strongest snowstorm I've seen."

Victoria nodded. "There were two strong storms last year as well, I understand. And there will be more next year." Again she scanned the faces; her last sentence had gotten their attention. "Would you like to know why?"

Now she had them; everyone nodded and/or said yes.

"It's because of something called 'fetch,'" she told them.

They became puzzled and attentive. One boy toward the back of the classroom called out, "Woof, woof!"

Victoria laughed, although she'd gotten that response before. "This is a different kind of fetch," she explained. "You can find it north of Canada. Would anyone care to try and guess what 'fetch' is?"

"A polar bear?" replied the boy who had woofed.

"Nooo . . . but it does affect polar bears. Anyone else?" A yellow-haired girl in the front row raised her hand, and Victoria gestured toward her.

"Well, if it's north, it might be a kind of ice," she said.

"Very close," Victoria told her, and the girl beamed. "In fact, it refers to a stretch of ocean in which there is *no* ice. Who knows which ocean I mean?"

Two students called out, "Arctic Ocean." Another offered, "Russia."

"Arctic, yes," said Victoria. "And Russia does have a long coastline on the Arctic Ocean. So now we have 'fetch,' which is ice-free ocean, and we have the Arctic Ocean. We need one more ingredient to cause these snowstorms: it's called the jet stream. What's the jet stream? Anyone?"

"Southwest Airline," said a boy off to her right. Others in the class laughed, as did Miss Yolanda.

Victoria, however, gave a little nod of approval. "Airliners do fly in the jet stream, that's true," she said. "And we'll talk about that in a few minutes. But for now, what you need to know is that the jet stream is a flow of air, way up in the sky, that goes around the Earth. Up until a few years ago, the jet stream was found about as far north as our border with Canada, and it blew from west to east. There were a few loops now and then," she made a little motion with her hand like a sine wave, "but for the most part its location was reliable. So was our weather. We didn't have monster storms like the ones that struck the east coast this past year. We didn't have very much snow here in Albuquerque. Places like Alabama and Mississippi and Florida stayed reasonably warm during the winter."

Here Victoria paused, to find out whether anyone would ask. *Please be curious*, she wished.

The question came, from the woofer boy and the yellow-haired girl. "So, what happened?" they blurted. Other students sanctioned this breach of protocol with cries of, "Yeah."

Victoria went to the white dry-erase board and pulled down the map that was rolled up above it. She passed her hand over the Arctic Ocean and said, "For thousands and thousands of years, this was frozen. Weather on Earth, especially here in the northern hemisphere, was stable. So was the jet stream. But in the past century, the Earth grew a little warmer. Not very much, only three or four degrees. But let's think about that."

She moved to the front of the desk. A clear spot on top of it invited her to sit down, which she did, to the consternation of Miss Yolanda, who objected only with a frown. "What is your name?" she asked the woofer boy.

"Miguel Dario," he replied, shifting around in his chair.

Immediately Victoria realized she had made a mistake in asking his name. She was an authority figure, after all, and he did not know her or fully trust her. Fortunately, his last name offered her a point of commonality.

"From Nicaragua?" she asked gently.

Miguel stared at her, and licked his lips. "Y-yes, my . . . grandparents. But how could you know that?"

Victoria found a warm smile for him. "I only guessed," she admitted. "But Ruben Dario is the national poet of Nicaragua. He is very famous there, and much loved."

"But . . . but how would *you* know that?" he persisted.

She shrugged. "I used to collect postage stamps when I was younger," she explained. "I had some from Nicaragua, including one set of stamps that showed Dario Park. I liked those stamps, and so I looked up the name Dario, to find out why he had been honored with a park."

Miguel relaxed, and looked around, a smile toying with his mouth. Miss Yolanda seemed more at ease, too.

Victoria said, "Miguel, your temperature, and the temperature of everyone else in this classroom, is about ninety-eight point six degrees. All of you feel good, right? But Miguel, suppose your temperature went up four degrees. How would you feel then?"

Miguel's lips puffed out as he exhaled. "Whoa, I'd be sick. Mama would take me to the doctor."

Do you get it? she asked silently, as she looked around the room. Yes, two or three faces had sobered in thought. There, another one is thinking. And Miguel, too!

"The Earth is sick," she said quietly. "And she has no doctors."

Victoria let that sink in. After half a minute of silence, the yellow-haired girl piped up. "Why can't *we* be the Earth's doctors?" she asked.

Victoria smiled her approval. "We can," she said. "We will all have to do our part. But like a doctor, we must first know the symptoms. I said the Earth is warmer now. What does that mean for the Earth?

A girl with braided black hair and skin the color of cappuccino spoke up. "The ice melts," she said.

"Exactly. The effect of temperature on the wind in the Arctic changes that wind. That, in turn, changes the jet stream. The more ice that melts, the more the jet stream is affected, the more the weather changes. But the process is slow. At first, only a little spot of ice melts, and exposes the ocean underneath. Now the wind blows, and instead of blowing over snow and ice, it now blows over water as well. The exposed water is called fetch. In this fetch, waves form. These waves crash against the ice, breaking it up and making it easier for the ice to melt. As more ice is broken up and melts, more fetch is created, more ocean is exposed to the wind, and more powerful waves form. Once it begins, the cycle of ice and waves and water will not end until the entire Arctic Ocean is open sea."

Victoria paused. She had spoken a little too long, and was starting to lose them. Already two students in back were looking out the window.

"This wind," she continued, "is the engine for the jet stream. Its air is warm because it is passing over water instead of ice. So the jet stream is warmer. Let's see what that means."

She got up and went back to the great map. "Remember," she said, "the jet stream flowed almost straight across the northern part of the United States, with only a few little loops? But now, with the increase in temperature, the jet stream has changed, too. Now it has very deep loops." Her hand made a series of parabolas across North America. "One of those deep loops brought cold air all the way down here to Albuquerque, and caused that snowstorm that kept you out of school."

Victoria could tell by their faces that she had them once more.

"That's why there's more snow and cold weather, even though the Earth is warmer," she finished. "The weather is loopy."

Their laughter gave her a brief satisfaction. If nothing else, they would remember that simple phrase: the weather is loopy. Perhaps it would trigger a curiosity about the rest of what she had told them.

Victoria moved back to the desk and sat down on top of it again. "Well, then," she said. "Questions?"

At first no one spoke up. Several seconds later, a dark-haired boy near the center of the room raised his hand, and she acknowledged him.

"How many points did you score?" he asked.

The question was not unexpected, but still she laughed. "Nine."

"That's all?"

"That's all I scored in the Olympic Games," she told him. "I also play in a league on North Island, and there I score about ten points a game. Any other questions?"

"How does the new jet stream affect airplanes?" asked the yellow-haired girl.

"Ah, good question," she said. "When the jet stream blew from west to east, airplanes flying from west to east could use it to help power the airplane. In doing so, they used less fuel, and arrived at their destinations quicker. But now, if the airplane is flying from west to east and the jet stream is blowing from north to south, or from south back up to north, it can't use the jet stream. In fact, sometimes the jet stream blows against the airplane. So the airplane uses more fuel, which in turn affects the air we breathe. It also costs more to fly in an airplane, and flights take more time. It's a lose-lose."

"All because of this fetch?" asked Miguel.

Victoria made a little face. "Well . . . not exactly. Fetch is a consequence of ocean ice melting. The cause of that is the Earth's fever. Remember, it's four degrees warmer now. We doctors—you and me—have to find a way to bring that fever down."

She cringed as she said it, for it was at best misleading and at worst a fabrication. The Arctic ice was not going to re-form. The glaciers were not going to reconstitute themselves. Humanity had to try to anticipate and deal with the future—with flooded coastlines and irregular weather patterns—as well as curb those activities that caused the Earth's fever in the first place. But she had to follow the Ecotect line, if she wished to continue working for them, and that line stipulated a change in society and commerce so radical that it would be catastrophic if done too quickly.

Sometimes she felt like a voice in the desert.

Miss Yolanda approached her, carrying a green plastic box for file cards, which she handed to Victoria. "The class would like to contribute today's lunch money to help in the efforts to protect the environment," she declared.

Victoria did not feel particularly gracious at the moment; nevertheless, she found a grateful smile for the children. "Thank you," she said. "Every little bit helps a lot. And as we say in New Zealand, *kia manawanui.*"

"What does that mean?" asked Miguel.

"It means . . . well, it's a way of saying, 'Keep on keeping on.' In other words, don't give up."

"What's in that box?" the yellow-haired girl wanted to know.

"Ah, this one?" said Victoria, as she slipped down from the desk. "I felt bad, because you all gave up your lunches today to help the Earth." She removed the lid from the box and turned it up so they could see. "So I brought chocolate cupcakes," she went on. "You can each have one."

A freckled boy with red hair spoke up. "But we're sixteen, and Miss Yolanda makes seventeen," he pointed out, adding hopefully, "But there are eighteen cupcakes."

Victoria grinned. "Don't I get one, too?" she asked.

*

The flight from Albuquerque to Denver took three hours to check in, pass security, and board; almost two hours of flight time, as the jet stream was running north to south; and another two hours fighting airport crowds and the usual insane rush hour traffic. The flight time made the other waits tolerable. Unable to check in to a window seat, Victoria settled for an aisle, and hoped the other two were not occupied by overweight middle-aged men who had to pee every twenty minutes.

The arrangement she found exceeded her expectations. Only the window seat was occupied, and that by a gentleman in his early forties, who had already dozed off. His dark blue suit was just expensive enough to look bespoke and yet still come off the rack. He hadn't even bothered to loosen his blue-green necktie. A businessman was he, then? But he had an outdoor complexion, and his tan did not come from a salon. A few streaks of gray gleamed in his medium-length brown hair, somewhat disheveled now that his head was leaning against the window. A laptop, presumably his, had been tucked into the bin on the back of the seat in front of him.

After stowing her travel bag in the overhead bin, Victoria sat down

96

gingerly, so as not to awaken him. Although she preferred the window seat, aisle was more than acceptable; it allowed her to stretch her long legs, and she didn't have to climb over others (and risk a gratuitous groping) in order to exit. She kept her seat upright, fastened the seat belt, and drew several relaxing deep breaths before tumbling into a meditative trance that soon became sleep.

The question drew her slowly back. She emerged blinking. The light tremor of her seat said the airplane had already taken off. Her ears adapted to the decrease in pressure. But the question—only one word of it had she heard, or perhaps it had only consisted of one word. She almost caught it, but not quite.

"Hello," he said, somewhat apologetic. "I didn't mean to awaken you."

The man in the window seat. His voice was mid-range, modulated, and masculine. She had the impression he had been studying her for a while.

She glanced at him. "How long . . .?"

"We've been in the air for about an hour now."

She yawned and stretched her legs.

"Basketball?" he asked.

She nodded. That's what he had asked a few moments ago. She shook her head, taking back the nod. Men tended to make that assumption about her, because of her height; that the assumption was accurate did not assuage her annoyance. As an opening line, it lacked originality. Worse, the worn silver ring on his third finger left hand suggested an ulterior motive for striking up a conversation.

She was about to tune him out when he said, "Forgive me. You probably hear that all too often."

"Rather a lot, actually," she responded, not quite against her will. She shrugged. "As it happens, I've played."

The man tilted his head slightly, examining her. "But you'd rather be known for your work." When she stared at him, astonished by his intuition, he went on, "Forgive me again. When you did not elaborate, I concluded you would rather talk about something else, if at all. Jeffrey Smith."

Not Jeff, she noted. Not the amiable sort in search of a quick and

97

anonymous tumble, then. Jeffrey made the conversation friendly, yet maintained the distance of a seat between them.

Following a brief hesitation, she took his proffered hand, and gave him her full name. "Smith," she repeated, wondering how many times he had signed it in a cheap motel.

"I thought of changing it to Smythe, but that seemed too pretentious. Australian?"

"Close enough," she said. "New Zealand."

"Turn the page," Smith said drily, mocking himself. "Read the next line. What brings you to this country, Ms. Chambers?"

Victoria laughed. "I work here, for Ecotect," she replied.

"Ah. My wife was with them, and other organizations . . ."

His voice trailed off, and he turned his head to gaze out the window. She wondered whether the direction of their talk had tweaked a nerve in passing. He grasped the ring with thumb and forefinger and turned it a few times.

Suddenly he turned back toward her, a smile just tickling the corners of his mouth. "I'm sorry. I . . . my wife died a few years ago."

Was that a lie, concocted to elicit sympathy? She issued a perfunctory, "I'm sorry."

His lips puffed out with his sigh. The sheen of moisture that had begun to cover his pale blue eyes slowly faded. "It's quite all right," he told her. "I've learned to edit my memories."

Now she believed him. She felt her expression soften of its own accord. "She was an environmentalist?" she asked.

"Oh, yes, quite." His eyes acquired a distant focus. "Yes, she did a stint with Greenpeace, blocking whaling ships. Sierra Club, Muir Society; Ecotect, although she did not stay with them for very long."

That raised Victoria's eyebrows. "Oh? Why not?"

"I'd . . . rather not say."

"You won't offend me, Mr. Smith."

"Ah . . . well . . . she was never specific. She just had the feeling there was something shady in the organization's hierarchy."

She flashed a grin at him. "Luckily, I'm not part of the hierarchy, then."

Smith seemed to relax, as if some hurdle had been cleared. "I told her she ought to be Secretary of the Interior, or head of EPA, but she just laughed. Said that's not where to power to affect lay. That puzzled me at first, but then she explained. The position in politics that gets the most coverage is First Lady. Oh, sure, the president receives a lot of ink and air time, and deservedly so. But aside from a few state visits hither and yon, his preserve is the White House and Camp David. The First Lady goes everywhere, from various councils to schools, to speaking engagements at universities. Yes, to cutting a few ribbons, but she makes speeches there as well." He sighed. "Well, it was a fine argument."

"From what little I know about this country's politics," said Victoria, "I'd say she had a valid point. May I ask . . .?"

Wrinkles appeared at the corners of his eyes, and she realized he was probably closer to fifty than forty.

"She spent a couple years in Flint, Michigan," he answered, speaking so as to avoid dwelling on the words themselves. "This was just before we met. It seems some of the effects were cumulative, as others sadly are finding out."

"Flint," she said flatly. "The water. I've read a study or two. In fact, that's supposedly part of my job—environmental specialist."

"Supposedly?"

"Mostly I'm sent to one place and another, gathering donations and trying to educate people," said Victoria. "Education is the most important bit. The problem with environmentalism is that people don't seem to grasp that it's all tied together. You can't solve just one problem, you have to address them all. And by you, I mean everyone on the planet." She felt herself getting too wound up; to relax, she took a deep breath. It pleased her to note that Smith was waiting politely for her to gather herself.

"The rise of the oceans will not stop, no matter what we do," she went on. "We have to account for that. Every country with a coastline has to account for it. Yet we're doing nothing. I'm not talking about sandbag barricades. The ocean will win that one. Even the dikes in the Netherlands are doomed."

"I fear you may be right," said Smith.

The airplane's speaker rousted them and the other passengers, instructing them to fasten their seatbelts and raise their seats to the upright position. Victoria realized she had no need to do either.

"Well, 'strangers on a plane,' and the trip was too short," said Smith. "I'd like to talk with you some more, Ms. Chambers, if that's all right with you."

Victoria masked her disappointment. *Here it comes.*

"If not, well, I understand," he went on. He withdrew a little black folder from his shirt pocket, and slipped a business card from it. With a simple Pentel ballpoint he inscribed something on it, and passed it to Victoria.

"I'm staying there with a friend," he explained. "This evening will be busy for us, catching up, and we have a lot of planning to do. Could you come to that address tomorrow evening? Around five, say. Take a taxi; I'll take care of the bill, and call you one when it's time to leave."

"I don't know," Victoria said truthfully. Her ears filled as the plane descended. She read the address aloud. "Four hundred on Eighth Avenue? I don't even know where that is. Downtown, I suppose." She tucked the card into a pocket of the black jeans she favored for traveling. "I'll . . . think about it."

He gave her a look that she was unable to interpret—a blend of puzzled amusement, as if there was something he had expected her to do that she had not done.

"Please do that," he said. "I imagine you've heard this before, but my intentions are strictly on the up-and-up. A talk over dinner and for as long as we've something to say, and then you return home."

"Hotel," she amended. "I live in Omaha. As I said, Mr. Smith, I will think about this."

The airplane's engines began to whine; they were about to land. Victoria closed her eyes to avoid giving anything away by her expression. Smith seemed genuine, which struck her as odd. Accustomed to fending off other invitations, she had begun this conversation on the defensive, a barrier his openness had quickly breached. As if he had breached others before? Or because he'd given her enough reason to lower it? As the plane landed and taxied along the runway, she decided she would pass on his invitation. Either it was too good to be true, or it concealed some darker purpose. Either way, it was meant to be avoided.

They parted company coolly enough, and he hurried off as if someone were waiting for him. Exhausted, Victoria trudged to the luggage belts for her suitcase, which she dumped into a storage locker after removing a few essentials. A walk of half a mile brought her to the taxi stand.

*

By the time Victoria checked into a Super 8 motel and chucked her overnight bag and suitcase onto one of the two double beds, eight o'clock had come and gone.

The lock and the deadbolt belied the thin walls; nearby she could hear a woman yelling in Spanish, a child crying, and a dog barking. The shower drowned out most of the noise, and she relaxed in the steam from the hot water. Perhaps too long, for her fingers were wrinkled when she emerged to dry off with one of the complimentary white coarse towels. She missed her little apartment on the outskirts of Omaha, where it was quiet and people grew flowers and shrubs, where her Prius hybrid awaited her attention. She hoped the sounds would abate eventually.

She debated whether to have a pizza delivered, but there was no way she could eat the whole thing, and the room accouterments included neither an efficiency cooler nor a microwave to accommodate leftovers. Dinner therefore consisted of a can of Coke and a bag of chips not long past the expiration date. The little bag was only half-empty when she fell asleep.

*

Victoria awoke to sunlight and to the sound of someone dragging a suitcase past her door. For a few seconds, her eyes refused to focus. Disorientation stabbed at her when they did; this was not the cottage by Lake Rotomahana, this was . . . what was it? She blinked. Memory and realization filtered in. A motel room.

Oh.

She sat up and dropped her feet to the carpet, and rubbed grains of sleep sand from her eyes. The clock on her Palmetto said she had an hour to check out, thirty minutes more to get to the Ecotect main office in the brand-new Mile High Marriott. Got up, trudged to the bathroom, prepped herself for the day. Dressed, an aqua pants suit with a cream blouse. Shod herself in casuals. A touch of foundation, a hint of blush, and a dab of lip gloss completed her look.

Bright sunlight made her eyes ache as she made her way to the motel office, dropped off her key card, and called for a taxi. Once inside it, she sat back for a moment to collect herself. Two more trips, she thought. To headquarters to report back to Michael and deliver the contribution from the schoolchildren, then back to the airport and fly to Omaha, to the tranquility of her apartment until the next public relations assignment. Her lips puffed as she exhaled, and told the driver where to take her.

Fifty minutes of dodging Denver traffic—four to five vehicles usually crossed an intersection after the light changed—brought her to the sparkling edifice known as the Mile-High Marriott. Like something out of *The Jetsons*, its spired height made it at 774 feet the city's tallest building. Reflected sunlight illuminated much of the surrounding neighborhood.

Albedo, thought Victoria. *The damned thing had the albedo of Enceladus.* She shrugged; Colorado was notorious for excessive expenditures where its buildings were concerned. She recalled the Veteran's Administration fiasco in nearby Aurora, and of course the aborted proposal to house some underage undocumenteds in a remodeled Denver Federal Center warehouse in suburban Lakewood. Not to mention the plans to install a retractable roof on Mile High Stadium for the Broncos. Now this.

Her neck ached as she gazed up at the top of the hotel. There was no way, she thought, no way the hotel could book all those rooms. They had to lease some of them out for commercial purposes. To Ecotect? What the hell was Michael thinking, headquartering the organization here?

Foreboding darkened Victoria's mood as she entered the lobby and found the floor information board that showed Ecotect offices located on the Sixtieth Floor. She stepped into the lift—she had to remember they were called "elevators" in the U.S.—and searched the panel for the number 60. The elevator was gauged to ascend no higher than the Fiftieth Floor. She exited the elevator and strode briskly to the registration counter.

The clerk was attired in a dark blue bespoke suit that went well with the indigo furniture in the lobby. His name tag read Keller. He was wearing an earbud. His pale underskin lent a touch of pallor to the tan he had acquired under a lamp. His gray eyes took her in, and she had the feeling he was examining her own sunlight tan with a bit of jealousy. First impressions, she thought ruefully. Aloud, she asked how she might reach the Sixtieth Floor.

"Whom did you wish to see, Madam?" Keller inquired, with what she recognized as forced courtesy.

"Michael Aspen of Ecotect," she replied, and introduced herself, adding, "He's expecting me."

The clerk's tone said he doubted that. "I'll just check, Madam," he said, and keyed the communicator at his counter.

"Not Madam," said Victoria, with some asperity. "Ms. Chambers will do nicely, thank you."

"Sorry, Mad—Ms. Chambers." He held up a finger for silence. "Ms. Hayes? This is the front desk. I have here a Ms. Chambers to see Mr. Aspen. Yes, I'll hold."

He continued to maintain an upraised finger while he waited. Victoria chafed under the delay. She found herself wondering about the penalty for hijacking a lift.

"Yes, still here," said Keller, listening. "I see. Thank you." To Victoria, he passed on some instructions. "You're to leave the parcel here. Someone will come down to pick it up."

"I need to see Mr. Aspen," Victoria seethed.

"That was not mentioned, Mad . . ."

Victoria dug out her Palmetto and speed-dialed Ecotect. When the receptionist answered, she said, "This is Victoria Chambers. I wish to see Mr. Aspen. Please clear me to come up."

"I'm sorry, Ms. Chambers, but he is unable to see—."

"He will see me right now," snapped Victoria. "Or he can find himself another public relations minion."

The receiver fell silent, as if she had been put on hold. Presently the communicator at the desk buzzed, and Keller enabled it, pressing a hand against his earbud to be certain of hearing clearly. For a few seconds he stood listening. Then: "Right away, Ms. Hayes." To Victoria, he added, stiffly, "You may use the express elevator."

Victoria resisted the urge to glower at him. "Thank you," she said, and walked away.

The interior of the express elevator had no floor buttons, only a pair that were labeled for ascent and descent. She touched a fingertip to ascend; the doors slid shut, and a moment later her stomach descended and her knees buckled. A light above the doors indicated the floor the elevator was passing. By the time it reached 20, her stomach had returned, though her knees remained bent. She hoped the elevator would not stop too suddenly, or Aspen would have to scrape her off the overhead with a snow shovel.

Not Aspen, she decided. That task would fall to Ms. Hayes. Aspen had probably just visited his manicurist.

The elevator gradually slowed, then stopped. When the doors opened, Ms. Hayes was waiting. A glossy-haired brunette, she was attired in a lavender pants suit that made her gender quite clear. She regarded Victoria with slightly narrowed lilac eyes, as if Victoria's visit was above her station. Victoria guessed she was wearing tinted contact lenses, and recalled that Aspen's favorite color range took in the lighter shades of violet. He must have hired for her looks, she thought, then chided herself for being unfair. As she followed Ms. Hayes to the Ecotect suite, she took in the lavish surroundings—a statue on a marble plinth here, a mural by Dali on the wall there, a sitting room to one side furnished with a plush sofa and armchair set and an equally plush carpet, all in turquoise and old gold, and all illuminated by state-of-the-art LED panels in the ceiling.

They reached the receptionist's office, where Ms. Hayes instructed Victoria to wait while she checked with Mr. Aspen. Victoria surveyed the shiny teak desk, ergonomic swivel chair on casters that she had no doubt rolled silently, the glistening laptop hooked up to a plasma monitor half the length of the desk, the thick curtains on the great window, drawn now to present a view of the city and the mountains beyond.

Finally, Victoria could stand it no more—her lips pursed in silent yet ferocious disapproval, stifling a groan. For a moment, outrage clouded her vision. She wanted to scream a protest at something or someone. Instead, she forced herself into a calm that would last at least until the door closed behind her when she entered Aspen's office.

Ms. Hayes returned, and made a desultory gesture. "You may go in now, Ms. Chambers," she said, her tone all business.

Victoria issued a perfunctory, "Thank you." After dipping into her handbag and pushing a button, she entered the office and closed the door firmly behind her.

She decided not to explode—at least, not right away. And throttling him would yield only a fleeting pleasure. She simply stood still, regarding him from across the room, her smile a veil.

"This is a pleasant surprise, Kiwi," said Aspen, coming round the desk to greet her. "How was your trip?"

"Arduous." A wave of her hand took in the entire office. "Michael, what's all this in aid of? Teak? Mahogany? Carpeting so thick it has to be mowed periodically?"

The questions halted his approach. His thick lips bowed in a frown. "I'm not sure I understand you," he said.

She glared at him for a few seconds, and saw him take a step back. "I think you understand me quite well," she fumed. "Is this, is all this, how you spend the money?"

Aspen's face reddened. "This is necessary," he snapped. "We have to present an image of respectability—"

"Oh, bollox! The environment isn't about money-gathering, it's about taking action to protect it and to help people deal with the changes in it. What have you . . . what has Ecotect actually accomplished? What?" This she punctuated with a grunt of disgust.

"You don't understand—"

"I *don't have to* understand," Victoria shouted. She knew she was losing it, but she didn't care, not now. This would be her last day with Ecotect. "I can observe. I see things, Michael, and I am quite capable of interpreting what I see." Again she waved her arm at the room. "What I see here is you living in luxury while sixteen children in fourth grade donate their lunch money to you. You *bastard!*

To her surprise, Aspen began his response in a dulcet tone, as if to conceal his true feelings in a wave of saccharine. "You just don't get it,

Kiwi. We've done nothing because right now there's nothing we can do. We have to wait until people wake up to what's going on in the environment around them. We want them to be good and scared. We want them to be terrified. Climate changes and unusually strong storms and rivers overflowing and waves flooding coastal areas are *exactly* the sort of thing we need. When people are frightened enough, they'll make demands of their elected officials, and those officials will have to turn to the experts. That's us! That's Ecotect! We'll be in charge. They'll listen to us tell them what to do. They'll obey! They'll follow orders!"

Victoria spat a word she didn't realize she knew.

Dominant now, Aspen moved from the desk and toward her. For one wild moment, Victoria thought he was going to attack her. But he diverted to the wet bar, where he poured single malt whiskey into a pair of crystal tumblers.

"You need a drink," he said calmly. "You need to relax and understand."

Her voice coarsened from shouting, she hissed at him. "I understand, all right. This isn't about the environment. It's about power. It's always been about power—gaining it and keeping it."

Aspen picked up the two drinks and approached her. "Of course," he agreed. "And power costs money. Access costs money. We pay politicians for access. When the time comes, we'll call in our markers. The environment will be so bad that they'll have no choice but to do what we tell them to do." He handed her a tumbler, and hoisted his own in a toast. "I want you to settle down and be part of it, Kiwi. You're our best fundraiser. *À votre santé*," he finished, and took a sip.

Victoria rolled her eyes. "*À la votre*," she said, the proper reply, and tossed the drink in his face.

"You bitch," said Aspen, to her rigid back as she strode toward the office door.

She whirled around, and reached into her travel bag to display her Palmetto. "It's all on here, Michael," she said evenly, back under control now. "Every word."

Aspen wiped his face with a bar towel. "Wait," he said, unable to quell the plea in his tone. "What are you going to do, Kiwi?"

She depressed the handle, and opened the door. "The right thing," she told him, and walked away without bothering to close the door.

Mentally she cringed, thinking Aspen would pursue her. Part of her hoped he would—he was in no shape to take her on physically. But another part of her hoped he would hold back; she disliked unnecessary trouble. By the time she reached the elevator door and pushed the call button, his office door had closed, with him inside. She permitted herself a tiny sigh of relief . . .

. . . and a sigh of regret. She did not know what she would do now. The answer to problems of climate and environment began with education, but she had no voice, no sanction. Nobody would listen to her; they had no reason to.

The elevator arrived. Swiftly she stepped aboard and pushed the button for the main floor, lest Aspen find a measure of courage and decide to stop her, after all. To try to stop her. When the doors closed and the elevator began to descend, she took a huge breath and exhaled audibly.

On the way down, she thought of her apartment in Omaha. With her out of a job, it became nothing more than a *pied à terre*, a waystop on her journey back to New Zealand, this time possibly to stay. A bitter taste filled her mouth.

The door opened. She emerged into the lobby. Keller gave her no more than a passing glance as she walked outside; evidently Aspen had not called down for her to be held there. She sat down on a bench at a nearby bus stop.

And there the shakes hit her. Meditative breathing techniques brought them under a semblance of control, but still she hugged herself. Tears formed in her eyes, but they had not the temerity to fall. She had at least that much control. She fished in the travel bag for a Kleenex, and dried her face. A taxi stopped in front of her, as the light had changed to red. It was free. She got up and touched the door handle, indicating that she wanted to climb in, and the driver nodded. She said two words, "Airport, please," and sat back.

Airport. Airplane. She had no idea where the inspiration had come from, but she found herself asking, "Can you tell me what's at four hundred on Eighth Avenue?"

The driver laughed. "That's the Governor's Mansion, Miss."

Her jaw dropped. Quickly she fumbled in the travel bag for the business card, locating it when her hand inadvertently struck something sharp. She had not examined the front of it before now, but there it was, with words in bold black letters against an ivory background. Four lines. His name in a larger font than the other three lines. Her heart stuttered, excited, as she read them over and over again.

VOTE FOR

JEFFREY T. SMITH

FOR PRESIDENT

IT'S NOT TOO LATE

Hope filled Victoria's heart, as did a possibility. "Take me there instead," she ordered, and felt her heart tug at her in anticipation. She'd be early . . . but that was okay, for they had much to talk about.

The Wrong Kind of Ship
By Gustavo Bondoni

"What in the world is that?" Nico said. The transmission was scratchy, distorted and completely unintelligible.

"I have no idea. The AI is analyzing it. So far, it's managed to tell us that the message repeats every 45 seconds, running on a continuous loop," Melisa replied. She closed her eyes and communed with the implant in her forehead, her curly brown hair swaying as she moved her head. "It also says that the speech pattern doesn't conform to any of the languages that we brought under with us."

"So, maybe a Topsider tongue?"

"The Topsiders are dead. Even if they aren't all gone, there hasn't been a radio transmission on the surface in a hundred and fifty years."

"This one isn't coming from the surface. Our triangulation places the source about two hundred kilometers west of us."

"Two hundred... there's nothing out there."

"There's something out there, and it's transmitting on in ELF. We only picked it up because we were scanning for solar activity that might affect our buoy antennas."

They listened to the scratchy voice for some moments more. As they tried to make sense of it, Melisa's face went slack, a sign that she was receiving info from Dinatta City's central AI.

"It's Chinese."

"Chinese? Like from the old political entity of China?"

"Yes."

"Amazing. Is there a City that speaks Chinese?"

"No. This dialect is called Mandarin and hasn't been widely spoken since the late twenty-first. The only City that had been founded back then was Amsterdam after the sea went over the dykes. Amsterdam speaks Flemaise."

"So, who is it? Some shadow city we've never heard of announcing its presence to the world? A submersible full of untouchables?"

"The AI says it can translate for us."

Nico shut up and gestured for her to play the translation.

The sound, like everything generated by the AI, came through in a clear sexless monotone. "People of Earth, this is a distress signal. We are visitors to your planet who have arrived on a mission from the star you call Tau Ceti. We come in peace. An accident has rendered our landing craft inoperable and we have sunk in the ocean. Any assistance that can be rendered will be greatly appreciated. The integrity of our hull is compromised, and we fear it will not hold out too much longer. We come in peace." Then there was a pause. "People of Earth, this is a…"

Their jaws dropped in unison.

*

The conference room was packed with as many experts as they could get to the Communications Pod at such short notice. Most of the people who might have been able to assist lived deep in the caverns, hours away from the crisis. The Pod, built above the ocean floor, was miles from the city proper.

The four people they'd been able to track down listened to Nico's summary and to the AI-generated audio in silence. Three of them were just off-duty comm supervisors but the fourth, Aldo Brinni, a visiting City Notable, actually had experience with traveling through water. Granted, it had been nearly three centuries before, and the machine that had carried him now resided in the Dinatta Historical Museum, but he was still the most authorized voice in the room.

Aldo removed his eyeglasses. They were strange, archaic things. At first Nico had believed that the man used them to try to stand out, to shock people he met. Only later did he realize that Aldo was so old that every corrective procedure had already been tried, and only glasses allowed him to see.

The old man rubbed the bridge of his nose. "They're screwed," he pronounced.

Heads nodded around the room, but to Nico's surprise, Melisa spoke up. She was the junior member of the discussion, invited only as a courtesy because she had been the one to receive the transmission. "What? We can't just let them die!"

"What do you suggest we do?"

"I don't know, but if you'd heard the original transmission you wouldn't just calmly sit there and say that they will die."

Aldo held up a hand to calm the offended supervisors, all three of whom were berating Melisa for her breach of protocol. "Please. I'm too old for this nonsense. In my day, we would let anyone with a valid idea speak up. Play the original audio."

Nico shrugged and did so. At the end, everyone looked at Brinni for guidance. "Interesting. Whatever entity recorded this sounds almost human. What did you think I would hear in this recording, young lady?"

"The voice sounds scared to me. Terrified."

Aldo thought about that, chewing on his white beard. "Hmm. Yes. I do believe you're right. But what can we do about that?"

"We need to go save them, of course."

"That much was evident from your outburst. What I meant was how do you propose to go about it?"

"The *NovaFreccia*—"

"Was disassembled when they brought it inside, and gutted. The thing in the Museum is just a collection of sheet metal, about as watertight as my latest bladder. There is not one single working submersible in Dinatta, and I believe none of the other Cities have any, either. Certainly not the ones that are in contact with us."

Nico nodded. He knew it, and Melisa did as well. After all, the Communications department was the first to receive news of anything happening in the other Cities.

"There has to be a way."

Aldo gave her a sad look, and then addressed the room. "If you can think of one, let me know. I'll see that you have the resources to do whatever it takes. Under one condition."

"What's that?" Nico asked.

"I'm not going out there. Traveling underwater is dangerous, and I'm not quite as young as I used to be." He stood with great difficulty and left the room.

Melisa, expression unreadable, went out the opposite door and returned to her post.

*

"That's insane, they'll throw you out of the nearest airlock."

Melisa remained steadfast. "He said that if I could think of a way

111

to do it, he'd get me the resources. Well, this is a way to do it. It would work, and it's not even that hard to do."

Nico sighed. Melisa was young, not quite thirty-five. She'd only gotten a position at the listening station because her Counselor team had warned that she would be unhappy continuing her post-doctoral degrees, and because her AI communing skills were excellent. But she still had so much to learn.

"They're *untouchables*. They chose to cut themselves off from all contact with civilized humans. We can't just call and ask them for help."

"They have submarines. Hell, they *live* in their submarines. That's the only thing that matters," Melisa replied. "They can reach a sunken craft in the middle of the ocean. Everything else is just meaningless social construction."

Nico heard himself gasp. It was an involuntary reaction that would have been shared by most citizens of Dinatta. The way society was structured was the only thing that had kept them alive when the climate changed. Untold billions had died, but the Cities had lived, even thrived in their underwater and underground forms because of a strictly controlled social order.

Minimizing the importance of that meant ignoring the achievements of a generation who'd sacrificed everything so their descendants could live. It wasn't just treason, it was closer to sacrilege.

He took a deep breath. There was no need to jump all over her. Allowances had to be made both because of her age and because she was his most valuable analyst.

"All right. I disagree with this, but it's not my call. Would you be willing to take this to Aldo?"

"Take what to Aldo?" a new voice boomed. The man himself strode into the room with a big smile on his face. "I thought I'd come over to see what you two were up to, and it's a good thing I did. You were probably just about to decide to leave me out altogether, and this is the most fun I've had in decades."

Nico said nothing. It was much too late to disavow any responsibility, no one would believe him if he tried—not after what Aldo had heard. He'd just have to pray that the man didn't actually order them both tossed into the sea. He also wondered, in that case, what would kill them first: the ice-cold water, the crushing pressure or just drowning. He decided that the pressure would probably kill them first, but slowly enough that they'd also get to feel the sensations of asphyxia and frostbite before they died.

"Melisa has a possible solution for the rescue of the aliens."

"Will it work?"

"Technically, yes, but—"

"Then I want to hear it. From her."

Nico was more than happy to let her take over. He'd been trying to protect her, an instinctive reaction whenever one of his team got in trouble, but he was relieved to let her talk for herself in this instance.

"I think we need to ask a submersible settlement for help."

The expected explosion never came. Instead of ordering them flayed, Aldo nodded thoughtfully. "It would work, but how do you plan on reaching them? Unless we have an ELF antenna I'm unaware of, we can't actually talk to them, can we?"

"We might. I caught a transmission just this morning that the *Pampas Humedas* is on the surface right now, repairing a leak. They're only about a hundred klicks away, and they might be monitoring standard radio transmissions."

The older man nodded. "They probably will. They like to know what the Cities are up to."

"So I was thinking we could talk to them and ask them to come here for a meeting."

"Untouchables never come to us unless we offer them something in exchange."

Melisa shifted uncomfortably in her seat. "That's what I wanted to talk to you about. Do you think the council would approve an exchange?"

Aldo chuckled. "I could get to like you. You have guts."

*

The untouchables smelled different, albeit not the way Nico had expected them to. It wasn't the unwashed and dirty smell of hundreds of people packed into a submarine but a subtle chemical odor, as if they washed their clothing with industrial cleaners.

113

The delegates from the *Pampas Humedas* sat on one side of the table, peering warily at the Dinattan representatives.

The untouchables—Nico knew he had to stop thinking of them that way lest his tongue slip at an inappropriate moment—had sent only three people: a tall, thin, silver-haired woman who was introduced as the Captain, and two younger men who seemed to be there mainly as muscle.

On the City's side of the table, things weren't much better. In addition to Nico and Melisa, they'd managed to convince one more member of the council to attend, a former shipmate of Aldo's who'd been instrumental in getting concessions to entice the untouchables to come.

"And you agree to machine spare parts for us for a year, just for listening to what you have to say? That is very generous."

"We do," Also said. Then he gave the captain a knowing look. "We have some experience with submarines, and we knew that the offer would get you here quickly. The favor we need to ask of you is time-sensitive."

It had worked. The Submersible habitat had arrived within twelve hours of receiving the message.

"Here is our current list of needs. How quickly can you produce them?" The Captain handed Aldo a plaz printout.

Aldo laid them aside. "Our shops can build you a complete new settlement in less than a month without breaking into their production schedule too severely, and most of that time will be to get the pieces transported somewhere where you can pick them up. Aren't you interested in why we called you here and what else we're offering?"

She gave him a level gaze. "Tell me."

Aldo gave a sign and Melisa played the recording, the original first and then the translation, explaining the circumstances it had been received under, and finishing with: "We've been dithering for over twenty-four hours, but the message is still transmitting, so there's hope we might get there on time."

The Captain sighed. "We picked that up. I thought it was just routine communication between two settlements that don't speak any of our languages. But your translation has made things a lot more complicated, hasn't it?"

"It has."

"Do you know anything else about it?"

Melisa answered. "The original transmission is in Chinese, which used to be Earth's major language a few centuries ago. Anyone coming in from space would likely have that in their database. It's possible they've been traveling since then."

"So, they travelled here from... how far away?"

"Twelve light years."

"Twelve light years away, and when they arrive, they can't navigate the atmosphere and they sink to the bottom of the sea? And no one on their interstellar craft can figure out how to pull them back out? Doesn't that sound a bit strange to anyone else?"

Silence met her question. It was the same doubt that most of the Dinattans had.

"So your solution is to send a settlement with nearly a thousand people, men, women and children, to find out whether it's legitimate or whether someone is setting a trap to steal our resources. And even if it's legitimate, which I don't believe for a second, has it occurred to anyone that these aliens might have come here to eat us or something?"

"Yes. Which is why it's important that someone go have a look. We're offering to send some of our people along, but more importantly, we're offering all the spare parts and upgrades you need for the next twenty-five years. And no questions asked, which means that if you decide you suddenly need to double the number of fuel cells aboard, you will receive them from us upon request."

The Captain sat back in her chair, suddenly wary. "That's even more generous than your last offer. Too generous, if you ask me."

Nico shared her surprise. Aldo hadn't seen fit to disclose the offer he was going to make to the untouchables. Beyond the sheer scale of the material promise, it would mean that the City would have a running relationship with the *Pampas Humedas* for the next quarter of a century. With an untouchable settlement. He wasn't sure how people would react to that.

Aldo shrugged. "We can afford it. We haven't been expanding as quickly as we were when those workshops were built. Our drilling equipment isn't wearing out anywhere near as fast as it once did. We have entire levels on the factory floor sitting idle." He held her gaze. "Besides, we're not asking you to send the entire settlement in to look. I know you have exploration vehicles. Send one of those in."

"How did—"

"I was on the *Pampas Humedas* some years ago. I spent time on most of the major settlements in these waters. The Mediterranean isn't all that big, you know. That was back when sea levels were still rising, and the City was new. We wanted to know what was moving around near us, and whether we'd have to expend resources on defense."

"I don't remember any people from the Cities."

"This was probably back before you were born. I'm not quite as young as I look," Aldo smiled.

The Captain's eyes widened. "You still have the Lazarus therapy here?"

"Of course. That's not technology you want to lose."

"Then that's my condition for taking your people to the site."

"Out of the question. Our initial offer is extremely generous. And it's also final."

Nico saw that she was torn. On one hand, she desperately wanted to live for centuries. It was written all over her face. But on the other, the service agreement would allow her people to rebuild their infrastructure and improve their quality of life beyond anything they'd imagined. From the ELF communications the Cities had been eavesdropping on for the past century, everyone knew that the untouchables were constantly running way behind on the maintenance curve. They didn't have the capacity to produce most of what they needed, so they were usually patching the most dangerous failures, always one step ahead of catastrophic failure.

Every once in a while, they'd intercept a frantic distress signal... and then there would be one less settlement in the Mediterranean. He shuddered to think what it must be like to sink to the bottom and wait for the pressure to overcome what the holds are designed for... or worse, for the power and the oxygen to finally run out.

Aldo went on. "But as you're interested in recovering Lazarus therapy for your people, perhaps we can continue this discussion after

116

we've rescued the aliens. How does that sound?"

"Hugely suspicious," the Captain replied with a tight-lipped nod. "But you seem to be holding all the cards. We'll do it."

Aldo gave her the faintest of smiles and returned her nod. Nico wondered what the hell he was up to.

*

The interior of the settlement did smell. It smelled exactly the way Nico would have expected. Overloaded, under-maintained air scrubbers couldn't deal with the humidity or the smell of over nine-hundred people locked in a floating can.

One thing that surprised him was the settlement's size. Instead of a claustrophobic warren of pipe-filled maintenance tunnels, he encountered a wide albeit dimly-lit corridor which had other passages crossing it at intervals of maybe twenty meters. The main causeway had to be at least three hundred meters long. It had to be impossible for this thing to float.

But as they led him across the wide street and into a smaller side lane, he felt the floor vibrate. The settlement lurched slightly and he knew they were in motion. After a lifetime in which the floor most definitely didn't move under him, Nico felt a bit sick.

Once more, he wondered how it was that he'd allowed himself to get dragged into this. Aldo wouldn't have been particularly angry had he refused, but when the council member had asked Nico if he wanted to go along, he'd acceded without even thinking about it.

Melisa, of course, hadn't waited to be press-ganged. She'd volunteered before anyone else had even been asked. Despite deep misgivings, he was also beginning to develop a grudging respect for her attitude. She might go against everything that had allowed the City to become a safe, stable environment, but she stayed the course even when it meant she had to risk her own skin to do it.

And now she was up ahead, asking questions of the local excursion vehicle driver who'd been assigned to take them to the aliens, a man named Eduardo. Nico picked up his pace.

"...you use the scrubbed carbon in the greenhouse levels?" he heard Melisa say.

"We mix it with other waste products as a fertilizer."

117

As the technical conversation continued, their guide led them into ever-smaller passages. Eventually, they came to a tube that was just big enough to admit one person. Their guide ushered them inside.

Suddenly, the air quality changed from stuffy to antiseptic. Eduardo gestured. "Welcome to the *Neptuno*. It's probably the oldest working vehicle anywhere on the planet... but it's also the best-maintained piece of the *Pampas Humedas*. We can halve our transit time by taking this one. The only real problem is that the sub is powered by an old-style fission reactor."

Nico froze. Only the fossil fuels that had made civilization on the Earth's surface impossible to inhabit were decried more stridently by teachers and society than nuclear fission. Everyone in Dinatta knew that even when things got really bad in the atmosphere fission was deemed a solution worse than the disease. People rioted in the streets to keep their governments from building fission reactors.

Of course, by the time the first fusion reactor came on line, the runaway greenhouse effect was too far along for it to make any difference.

Eduardo saw his face and gave him a reassuring smile. "This reactor has been running for hundreds of years without a glitch. We overhaul it every couple of decades, and it's shielded by a lot of lead. There is really nothing to worry about."

Nico decided to worry anyway, but he moved forward again as the man continued his explanation.

"The reason it's a problem is that fissionable material is no longer being produced anywhere, so we have to make periodic visits to the surface to get it. Fortunately, there's a big stockpile near the Arctic Sea that no one is using. We go there every few years to resupply."

Melisa's face lit up. "What's the surface like?"

"I haven't been there. My job is to drive submarines, I leave exploration to people who are actually crazy enough to do it."

The irony of a man who operated a nuclear-powered vehicle pontificating about sanity was, clearly, lost on him.

"How long will it take us to arrive?"

"At top speed? About ten hours. At least we have good sleeping quarters for while you wait."

"Sleep?" Melisa said. "Do you think I'd go to sleep during my first submarine trip? The City might never let me do this again. When do we leave?"

"Just as soon as…"

Nico let them get out of earshot and stopped by one of the bunks Eduardo had shown them. The last two days had been a nonstop grind, and he was utterly exhausted. He had few qualms in sleeping through his first submarine ride. Maybe that way, he could stop thinking about the fission reactor poisoning them all with its radiation.

*

"We found it," Melisa said, nearly jumping with glee. "It's caught on a ledge. They were extremely lucky not to keep sinking. They're only about fifty meters down – pressure isn't terrible down there."

Nico sighed. Even after his nap, it had been a long four hours before they managed to locate the source of the signals. The control cabin wasn't big enough for three people, so he'd let Melisa assist Eduardo in the search while he read electronic status reports on the large screen in the passenger seating area. "Is there anything I can see?"

His two shipmates emerged from the control center. "We've patched the sensors into the screen. We'll all be able to see much better from here," Eduardo said.

The first image that appeared was almost completely black, some darker and lighter shadows were faintly visible, but it might have been a trick of the monitor. "That's the image in the visible spectrum. We're still too far away for the floodlights to illuminate it effectively.

"Now this is an overlay of thermal imaging."

A triangular outline appeared, a very light green color.

Eduardo continued. "There's clearly something there. The final image we have available at this distance is a radar and sonar composite scan."

The triangle on the screen fleshed out and became… a triangle, but one that represented some kind of wedge-shaped vehicle as opposed to a fuzzy blur. It showed striations and other geometric shapes. There was no doubt that someone or something had built whatever they were looking at.

"I'll have the computer clean this up for us. It's not as good as a city

AI, but it should help us get a better idea of what it is we're dealing with."

The image in front of them blurred as the computer performed its magic. When the process was complete, the image was barely recognizable as the geometric blur they'd been viewing through the raw feed. It had coalesced into the image of a machine unlike any Nico had seen before. If the communication could be trusted, it was a machine that had descended from space.

The basic arrowhead shape was now festooned with tubes and panels—some visibly damaged—with antennae pointing out in various directions, and pods and bulges that appeared to have been grown in place.

"So what now?" Nico asked, attempting to keep his fear under control.

"It's your decision. I don't see anything immediately threatening, so if you want to go closer, that's what we'll do. Or we can transmit the audio you brought."

"All right, transmit."

Eduardo pressed the button which activated the sub's ELF antenna and sent out the newly created message which simply stated, in Chinese, that help was at hand and asked for instructions on how to proceed.

The response was nearly immediate. One moment, the endless loop of the repeating distress call was droning on like a carrier wave and the next, there was a new message, choppy and rushed-sounding, but unmistakably different.

They waited for Melisa's implants, updated with the best translator of Chinese available to Dinatta's AI, to make sense of the message.

"Thank you. Approach. Our boarding appendages are adaptable. Thank you. Approach…"

"They do like looping audio, don't they?" Nico said. He suddenly felt enthusiasm for what they were doing, and it made him think. Why had he come so far if he didn't really want to be there? At first it had simply been a question of being on duty when Melisa made her discovery. Then defending his teammate. Finally, when asked to volunteer for this phase of the mission, he'd been unable to tell Aldo to go to hell. What he'd wanted to say was that he had lived his entire life in the City, and liked the stability and structure that it brought him.

But now, looking at the machine on the screen, he felt something stir within him. He still wasn't convinced that it was an alien craft. It was probably human, and there had been some problem with the translation. But whatever it was, he wanted to have a look at it for himself.

Eduardo was looking at him expectantly. "So, what should we do?"

Melisa spoke up. "We'd said we would check in with Dinatta for help in interpreting the response. They have the ELF antenna the Captain lent them."

"I think the message is pretty clear. There's no real need to check in. Let's go see what that thing is," Nico said.

Melisa looked up, surprise evident in her features. Then she smiled and gave him a nod. "Yes, sir."

*

The people on the other ship were true to their word. The precaution of having them hook the pressurized access tube to the airlock was unnecessary, as the adaptable tube matched perfectly and no water rushed in, which is what Nico was expecting after all the back and forth over the ELF.

The tube wasn't illuminated, and it was empty. As part of the negotiations, the submarine team had asked to be allowed to board the stranded vessel before allowing anyone to cross over. Their interlocutors had accepted immediately.

What they hadn't told the other crew was that there were only three of them on the sub, which meant that only Eduardo would remain aboard during the expedition. If it was a trap, they wouldn't have a whole lot of backup.

The tunnel was dark, and the air emanating from it was cold, perhaps ten or fifteen degrees less than the air on the sub. Nico watched his breath condense in the beam of his helmet light and wondered why he wasn't a more afraid. Then he shrugged—or was that a shiver?—and walked on. If he hadn't, Melisa would have probably tossed him aside and gone on alone. She was truly eager to see what lay at the other end of the tunnel.

A small room with thick doors on either side, probably an airlock, was the first thing they encountered. It looked just like a human construct might look, except for one thing: though the outer door was round, the inner door was a strange shape. It was much wider than it was tall, about two meters by fifty centimeters. It was placed fifty centimeters off the ground, and was the first sign they'd encountered that their hosts might not be shaped like them.

The door forced them to adopt a crouching high-step to enter the next chamber.

This one was much bigger. Their helmet beams were lost among the shadows, but the room seemed to be filled with oblong bed-shaped objects on stilts, about waist high. It must have been some sort of rest chamber, Nico concluded.

"You walk around the room that way, I'll go this way," he told Melisa. "If you come to a door, let me know, and I'll join you. I'll do the same."

She nodded. "I wonder where they are."

"This ship isn't that big. We'll find out pretty soon. I hope they're all right, because I doubt the first aid kit we have on the sub is going to be much help."

"So you're finally convinced that they are aliens?"

"We'll see," he said, and began his walk.

The room turned out to be triangular in shape and large enough that it probably occupied most of the free space in the shuttle. They met at the opposite end from the doorway they'd entered through. "No luck?"

Melisa shook her head. "Not even cracks in the walls which might have been hidden panels."

"Maybe we're looking in the wrong place. Let's check the floor."

They began to walk through the center of the room, beams focused on the metal deck between the beds.

"Guys?" Eduardo's voice crackled through Nico's headset. Melisa, of course, didn't need the cumbersome gear; her implants took care of comm duties. "Just got a transmission from our friends. Beaming it over."

Melisa allowed her implants to translate. "They say that we've

122

found them and are walking among them."

"Among them? There's no one here."

"They say we're right beside them."

Nico looked around. Melisa did the same. Were the aliens invisible?

Suddenly, she gasped and crouched over one of the beds, and then put her ear beside it. "There's some kind of fan running here." She shook it. "Oh, my god. Come look at this!"

Nico hurried over to see that what had looked like a solid plastic rectangle was now filled with bubbles and light. He knew exactly what he was looking at; no one who'd spent time in the communications tower of any City would have been ignorant of it. "Bioluminescence!"

"I thought so, too... but that means..."

They both looked down at the prism beneath them. A mechanical body for some kind of microbe intelligence?

Eduardo's voice came through again. "Another transmission."

"They're asking us to be careful when we move them. They say it's better to push gradually than to shake them. They're also asking how soon we can start moving them to the sub."

Eduardo said: "I guess you must have found them. What do they look like?"

"You're not going to believe this. They're—"

The ship lurched. Nico was thrown to the floor, and Melisa fell beside him, but got back to her feet immediately. She helped him up. "It must be slipping off the ledge. Come on, we have to leave before..."

The second movement was more violent than the first. They were thrown across the room. Nico landed hard against something solid which knocked the wind out of him.

"I had to disconnect the tunnel," Eduardo's frantic voice said. "I'm sorry but it was leaking too much. I hope you're all right in there."

The ship began to move and Nico prepared himself to die. Even if the alien craft managed to seal its own lock, the pressure would soon overwhelm it. But he wasn't expecting to survive that long. Surely the disconnected tunnel would flood the ship.

But there was no sound of water.

So the ship, dislodged from its ledge would sink to the abyss.

"It's all right, Eduardo. We knew this was dangerous." Nico turned off his comm. He didn't want his last moments filled with chatter.

The craft began to accelerate, but something was strange. He must have knocked his head against something because every sense in his body was telling him that the craft was moving *upwards*.

And then it accelerated very hard and he was crushed against the floor. Blackness soon followed.

*

Nico woke in the arms of a cold metal spider. It seemed to be built entirely of sharp edges, most of which were burying themselves into his body at different points.

He struggled to get free, but there was no chance. The metallic arms held him in a viselike grip.

He tried to look around, but all he could see was the chamber floor. A humming filled his ears, which gradually changed pitch until it formed words.

"We understand there may be some discomfort," a metallic voice said. "We are inexperienced in the science of immobilizing humans." The language was perfect, unaccented Standarde, the tongue of the City-dwellers and even of most of the untouchables.

Nico tried to speak, sputtered and then managed to get his voice working. "Why would you need to immobilize me? Surely you can confine me somewhere while you do whatever it is you're planning?"

There was a pause, and then the humming returned, followed by words. "Our analysis of transmissions from your world indicated that damaged humans should be immobilized. You were damaged in the rescue. You are leaking fluid. If our immobilization is incorrect, please let us know what to do."

"You need to release me."

He crashed into the ground as the spider arms retracted at incredible speed.

But the drop was short and he already ached all over. What was one more bruise?

"What now?"

Nico nearly laughed in spite of the seriousness of his plight. "Let me catch my breath, and give me a few moments."

He made it to his knees and looked around. As far as he could tell, the room was constructed entirely of what looked like black marble. The walls he could see were semicircular, but one side of the room ended abruptly in a bank of complex machinery. There didn't seem to be anything immediately life threatening going on, although it was difficult to judge.

He took stock of his injuries. Scrapes and bruises seemed to cover his entire body, but there didn't seem to be too much actual damage. Of course, it would be a good idea to check that whatever had knocked him unconscious hadn't given him a bad concussion. A deep cut on his leg, seeping blood probably accounted for the leaking fluid his hosts had seen.

"Is my companion all right?"

"We aren't certain. It hasn't responded yet."

"Can I see her?"

The machinery on the other side of the room receded into the walls as fast as the one holding him had. He winced as Melisa dropped to the floor face first, and limped over to her.

He felt her neck for a pulse and was relieved to feel a strong beat. "Can you bring me a glass of water?"

A piece of the floor beside him seemed to melt and a glass cylinder of clear liquid ascended from it. It had no smell, and didn't harm his finger when he dipped it in, so he assumed it was water. Nico took some in his hand and dripped it onto Melisa's face. After a few moments, she sputtered and opened her eyes.

"What are you doing?" she asked, glaring at him and looking around in confusion.

"Trying to revive you," he replied, moving away so she could see their surroundings.

"Revive? What..." she shook her head, clearing it. "We were sinking. How did we get away?"

"I'm not really sure, but I am sure we didn't sink. Our friends' friends must finally have mounted a rescue. How are you feeling?"

Melisa paused and took stock, then she winced in pain and held up her arm. "I think I have a broken wrist. Or maybe sprained. Other than that, I think I'm OK."

"Good," he smiled. "And the wrist is even better. Our hosts want to learn how to immobilize damaged humans."

"Our hosts?"

"Hello. Welcome," the vibrating voice said. "We are happy to see that you are responsive again."

Melisa looked at him. "Is that what I think it is?"

"Yes. But I want them to do something about that wrist before we talk to them."

It only took a small amount of explanation before the floor secreted a layer of flowing metal that wrapped itself around Melisa's wrist and hand and then seemed to shrink wrap around its contours, leaving the fingers free and solidifying around the rest.

Melisa tapped it. "Pretty solid. I hope we can get it off once I heal."

"It is simple to remove, we will ensure that your medicals receive the necessary instructions."

She turned to face him. "Nico, where are we?" For the first time, she didn't look quite as excited by the possibility of adventure.

"I think I know, but we should probably ask." Out loud, he said, "Is there any way you could show us our current position?"

The black walls of the domed room they were in disappeared, replaced by a perfectly-rendered high-definition image. "This is the position."

Melisa grasped Nico's arm. She gasped with pain—she'd forgotten her wrist was injured—but he ignored the sound. His entire focus was on the blue sphere floating above his head. Clouds swirled over the Mediterranean, and over much of the rest of Europe, testament to the constant tropical acid rain that lashed the continent.

"We're in space?" she asked, gripping harder.

"It looks that way."

"Crap," she said. Melisa had turned pale.

Nico nearly laughed out loud. He'd expected her to be delighted. After all, this woman had dragged him halfway across the sea, ignoring both logistics and convention to do so, just to see something new and escape the city. As recently as the access tunnel to the alien craft, she'd been willing to push him aside if he dared slow her down.

But all of that had been underwater. Having dozens, or hundreds of meters of insulation above one's head made most people feel safe. Radiation couldn't penetrate the seas, and the weather that made life impossible on the surface was felt as gentle currents down below. For some, the underground caverns were even better.

But now, they were presumably out in orbit, surrounded not by an atmosphere that might be dangerous but wasn't immediately lethal, but by the hard vacuum of orbital space.

Nico should have been terrified, but for some reason he wasn't.

"We'll be all right," he told her. Louder: "Thank you. That's quite a view. So, what happens now?"

"We need to make contact with your Cities. We've managed to study the current layout of your society and concluded that it has changed considerably with regards to what we studied before setting out. Our initial attempt to land on the surface met some unexpected weather conditions. That was the mission you rescued."

"Did all of the… people survive?"

"All the segments were viable for reassimilation, yes."

"I'm sorry?"

"Perhaps it is best if I show you."

The image around them dissolved and a corridor formed in one side of the room. Nico noted with amusement that it was the same size and shape as the one on the shuttle, indicating that perhaps the plasticity of the alien technology wasn't absolute.

He walked through, and then followed the corridor to another door that led into a huge chamber. Machines skittered this way and that, and there was an enormous tank in the center of the room. The tank seemed empty, but had a light greenish hue.

"Welcome," the vibrations said. "I thought it might be easiest to show you what we are. Observe the liquid in front of you."

A streak of bioluminescence crossed the tank.

"That is us." There was a pause. "And we, in turn, are part of a much larger entity, an entire ocean of thought. The units you rescued were part of us, separated out into transport capsules for ease of surface exploration. It's the smallest amount of our matter that can be separated and still retain self-awareness and the necessary intelligence."

Nico stared at the tank, stunned. "How did you build this?"

"Over millions of years, we have managed to find ways to manipulate matter. Once we built automated machines that process accelerated. But now it is us who need to ask some questions, and to do that, we need to know how to contact an official envoy from your planet."

"We don't have a centralized government. You'll need to speak to each City separately. What do you need from them?"

"Colonists. We're offering a huge continent and the technological base for spreading to the stars in exchange for the use of your oceans."

"We all live under the ocean. It might be hard to try to convince them to negotiate."

"Will you help us?"

"Yes. With one condition. I want to be one of the colonists."

"Done."

He heard Melisa gasp behind him and turned to face her. "Want to come?"

She shied back. "I need to think about it."

Nico smiled to himself.

Pelagus
by Mike Adamson

People once said forty days and nights of rain was enough to flood the whole world, and today this makes us smile, because it's been raining for forty *years.*

In the equipment bay I feed myself into a survival suit with the practice of many years. Brilliant orange, with breathing gear, floatation system, radio locator beacon, light. The name *Lytton, K* is stencilled at the breast--my suit, made for me, Kira Lytton, in the workshops below. The suit will keep me alive for 24 hours if I'm ever unlucky enough to be separated from this metal island on which we journey.

Drift Station *Pelagus* was built in the last generation before Earth became uninhabitable. She was conceived as a self-contained community of scientists with direct access to the planetary ecosystem at the most intimate level, while in permanent contact with the cities out at L5. She would drift forever on the oceanic gyre, wander the world without need of propulsion, send back data without pause, so that perhaps one day the supercomputers up there in space would understand the mechanism of the global balances well enough to repair them.

This was the plan, but plans don't always work out. Oh, we're wandering the world, we're sending the data, but we were never supposed to be trapped here--isolated, a community cut off from the human race. Our third native generation will be born in the next few years, and the scientists and engineers who crewed this station when it was launched are now...well, *old.*

I've been coming up here to the flightdeck since I was ten years old. We all do, it's a rule of the community--every day a small group of us go up top to see the world outside, to experience it; once a month for any individual. It terrified me then and it terrifies me now, but I understand the necessity and make myself do it. This is the planet Earth in AD2132, it is what our ancestors made of it, and we suffer the curse of their attitude.

The gentle motion of the vast platform is something we're born to; our elders say if we ever leave *Pelagus* we'll have severe disorientation until we adapt to a world that's *not* moving. For though the platform weighs 390,000 long tons, the forces of the ocean cannot be resisted; the great swells of this endless storm exert terrible stresses upon the tremendous pylon that supports the habitation dome sixty meters above sea level.

I go up from the standby lounge with Kirby, one of the pilots who hasn't flown his aircraft in twenty years: the weather was too bad for too long, and now the aircraft are unserviceable. With us go Kinsela, a biologist, and Delia, a kid my own age who has become a meteorologist. We all follow in the paths of our elders, there's no option. Only in our spare time can we write or draw. The station that is our life consumes all else.

In the elevator, we double check our survival suits with their compact oxygen rebreathers. The air out there is now too poor in oxygen, too rich in carbon dioxide, to support human life for more than a few minutes. Forests are recovering all over the southern hemisphere at tremendous rate, and eventually they'll correct the gas balance--but not without our help. The ocean, which was responsible for the majority of the process, has been largely dead for half a century.

When I was younger I complained bitterly that I had no wish to go outside--ever. But we grow up quick here, we understand our realities. And nothing brings home to you how broken the world is better than stepping out of the hanger onto the old landing pad area.

We've all done it many times; going through the ritual of the safety tethers, checking each other's rebreathers, harnesses and seals, is second nature. When we've all confirmed we're ready, Kirby thumps a big green contact on a wall panel in the small exit lock alongside the hanger where the three helijets wait forlornly for missions that will never come, and we take hold of the safety rail, waiting for it....

The wind comes around the door and hits us with the worrying hands of a demon, slapping and tugging at our suits. When the door has gone back, the wan, blue-gray daylight seems infernal compared to the 5000°K artificial light we're used to, and we squint into the gloom as we brave the gale. The ocean is a thunderous breathing below us. I remember, the first time I came out here I thought some monster was below, wrapped around the station, roaring ceaselessly.

130

We step out into the fury of the Southern Ocean and it seems all sanity is left behind. The wind would lift us from our feet if it could, and we stagger along the safety rail with both hands on the metal. The suits and gloves are thick and tough but I know we'll feel the cold soon all the same. What irony--*warming* created the imbalance whose lower end we now endure!

Ten meters from the door we cling tight to the rail at the edge of the landing pad and look upon the ocean. We lift our eyes to it slowly, not because we don't know what it's like, but because we fear to see it without armor-glass between us and it. Rain squalls march across the heaving black sea like the tentacles of some hidden kraken, while lightning makes purple flickers along the horizon and whitecaps torn from the waves are racing sheets of foam. Those waves are the great rollers of the Circumpolar Convergence--the West Wind Drift of old-- and they're mountainous. Some reach halfway to the underside of the platform.

To look on this spectacle with the eyes of a child was the most frightening thing I ever did. I was in shock and denial for days. The human mind has a way of handling terrible things, however, and I got over it. The simple fact I understood what a storm is and had already watched the sky from the impersonal peace of the protected interior helped.

Some found it exhilarating, and I tried to be like them. Each time I made myself go that bit further. Eventually I reached the outer edge of the landing pad, where it overhangs the periphery of the hundred-meter hemisphere of the station's upper arc, and could look down at the churning ocean.

Fear is an old companion: horrified nightmares about the black deeps beneath us, about the storm one day overcoming the technical mastery of the station and sucking us down into cold oblivion. This is what it is to be born and live every day adrift on the face of the vortex.

I've come to look upon this monthly meeting with reality as the most valuable thing we do. It's like the Martian settlers climbing out of their underground cities to look at the pink sky and the desolation, to remind themselves of where they really are, beyond the bubble of Earth they took with them. This station is our bubble of an Earth that's gone, and we are as much wanderers as any who travel the planets.

I tell myself this as I look down at the terrifying tract of water, whose wave crests march out of the west, whose deep mass-flow propels the station; and I look up through the rain that suddenly pelts across my suit and faceplate. This is daytime, and beyond those flying thunderheads is a blue sky I've never seen and the sun that's roasting this planet alive.

But, just maybe, today, we'll break our record. That's what I say, and as the mathematician who worked out where we've been wrong before, it's my call to make.

We'll escape from the Convergence, and our sun *will* shine for us again.

*

The storm has been blowing since my father was a kid. The entire southern hemisphere is affected--an expansion of the circumpolar gyre, which developed into an endlessly regenerating system of storms in all three oceans. Our theorists have suggested it's the result of the wholesale melting of Antarctica's icecap: the appearance of a thick lens of fresh water overlying the ocean as far north as 45° south, mimicking the conditions of the early Earth when the oceans were just forming.

I saw the math for this proposal when I was younger and I study it every day. Apparently, there was a time before knowledge implantation. A hundred years ago people had to learn to understand maths one concept at a time--no wonder so many of them couldn't do it. Instead of symbols I see relationships; the symbols are merely a somewhat clumsy way of expressing them.

These are the truths of life. I let my mind blank as I lean against a tiled wall in the crew showers, enjoying the hot spray that soaks the cold from my body. The others are done already, now I have the bay to myself, and it seems I take longer to pull myself together than usual. I should be excited: today is the day we attempt the Grand Maneuver--completing a month-long tacking operation to put us into the root stream of the Humboldt Current. It will carry us north along the coast of South America, and away from the Convergence at last. But we've tried before, been disappointed, and this endless orbit of the southern continent has been our reality for so long, I can't quite imagine escaping from it.

Soon I shut off the water, hear it gurgle away to the recycling tanks a deck below, and begin to towel in the warm, humid air. I *am* excited, I realise, more than I've let myself know--and there lies the churning fear in the pit of my stomach. Not childhood fears of the dark depths, but the entirely adult terror of being wrong for no reason I'll ever understand. It's the not understanding I'm afraid of, because our whole existence is a bid to understand.

I dress in my uniform jumpsuit with an economy of motion beyond my years, never imagining an eighteen-year-old should be any different. I talk like an encyclopaedia, am absorbed in our task, and it's only when my grandmother speaks of life before all this began that I feel how strange our world has become.

My grandmother is the commander of *Pelagus* Station. Doctor Virginia Lytton is 76 and has carried the weight of the world on her shoulders for the 112 crew she started with in 2090. Maybe good forethought saw the sex ratio of the crew more or less balanced--or just dumb luck, because when the storms erupted all over this planet, making physical contact with the space cities near-impossible, we became a close-knit community. A city adrift, and a microcosm of the human experience. When the Lagrangian stations declined to send shuttles into the thick, treacherous weather anymore, we knew we were on our own. It wasn't long before a next generation began to appear.

My father, Doctor Roger Lytton, was born a few years into the mission and like all the others grew up at the knee of the scientists. I came along only after we became trapped in the Convergence. Before then, *Pelagus* had wandered the gyres of every ocean more than once, sometimes seeing the sun and blue skies through the endless grey, and the brown skies when great winds stripped the denatured soil from the continents and flung it at the sea.

I can imagine the shock, the day they knew we were trapped in the far southern latitudes…when the deep tug of the next current the station must enter was simply not there. The deep sails were trimmed but the expected shearing action was not encountered. From that day onward, any hope of an occasional visit from space was over.

133

I know what they did wrong. I know where the modelling failed, and today we'll know if I'm as good as I think I am.

Oh, I'm so scared.

*

The bridge is the place I'm most at home. I step through the hatch and am greeted with the lazy hails of the duty watch. Toby Garrett is current Officer of the Watch and nominally has command. He monitors the uplink to Armstrong City, when we can get a signal at all. He has the engineering team under him, and the science crews liaise as needed.

The bridge is a wide control room at the apex of the dome, and armor-glass windows look out on the terrible seascape. Lights burn around the clock. Displays glow overhead and on consoles, and I stand before the master ocean plot. This is a digital screen the size of a wall, displaying a whole-Earth chart. The marker of our present position is as far north as we've seen in my lifetime. Seventeen days ago, we raced close to the latitudes of New Zealand, and ached to see the Land of the Long White Cloud, hundreds of kilometers below our northern horizon.

"I thought I'd find you here," comes my father's voice, and I turn with a wan smile, taking his momentary hug. "They'll all be coming up in time for the turn."

"You're confident?" I ask in a whisper.

"Aren't you?" He rubs his whiskered chin, shrugs and says softly, "I know, I know. The one who comes up with it is always the last to be certain."

I go to a console and pull up a display, my hands passing through the digital graphics in the air. The water masses surrounding the station appear in softly glowing colors. "It's the fresh water lens, it's deeper in these latitudes than we ever imagined. There's nothing else to explain the pressing away of the origins of the northward current. The water mass we need is under it, deflecting north before rising to feed the Humboldt Current. If we can snag it in the next hundred-fifty kilometers, we can make enough northing to avoid going aground on the coast of Chile, or being sucked southward again."

My dad puts an arm around my shoulders and smiles that special smile just for me. "There's plenty of trench under us on that stretch. Once we're into the current there's no way we'll go aground."

"If we do...."

"We'll strand fast and the sea will batter this station to wreckage." He speaks in a bare whisper, because we've been over this many times. *Pelagus* can't afford to ever touch bottom; she was named for the free-swimming life of the old oceans, and is only viable when she's riding before current and wind. To be driven onto a lee shore and held there is her death-knell--and ours. Without this station, there's no survival on the bleak and alien planet Earth has become. Could the space colonies reach us with a rescue attempt? Perhaps they'd try, but....

"It's there, I know it," I whisper, cancelling the display and bringing up the glowing sigils of the expressive math. "The salinity variable is the only one that makes sense. Temperature penetration to the deep water will take thousands of years, that can't be behind it. We'd have to talk about change in the rotational period of the planet or a geographic barrier to flow, and we know neither can be correct, so--"

"Let it happen," he whispers. "The entire science staff has signed off on your theory, we've been working toward it for two years."

Two years of hard work based on my reasoning. I've watched the engineers battle the sea to modify the station's drag system--she can sail before winds by unfurling sails below the dome, but she also sails on the *currents* by lowering 'propulsion area' into deeper waters. And there lies the difficulty.

The currents heading where we need to go are a good 300 meters deeper than they used to be. To get the 'water sails' down there, the hoists needed to be reworked to pay out a half-kilometer more cable. This doubles the odds of a cable snapping under load--if we lose the sails, it'll take us two *years* to rebuild them, cannibalising parts of the station, and all the time we'll be at the mercy of the wandering patterns of the ocean.

This is why we became lost. The currents haven't ceased to flow but they *have* moved. The sims couldn't account for it. The team battled the problem for many years while we were locked into the Convergence and lost our ability to send data on the rest of the oceanic system. Scientists used to say the Southern Ocean was the heart of the world's weather machine; in that much we're in a good place to be useful, and the data bursts we've been able to get through to the colonies certainly helped.

But what about *us?*

I never imagined my epiphany would carry such a weight of anxiety. The numbers looked so perfect, so clean and logical when I first glimpsed them and innocently blurted them out to the scientists I work with. They saw the sense of them; we ran the sims again and this time found the current. We ran them a thousand times, adjusting for uncertainty, and in a statistically significant majority of cases, we caught the current and made it into the South Pacific. Then we ran sims on the engineering work needed, and again it looked good, though the uncertainties were wider.

Now the hoists, located at the bottom of the station core, among the cathedral-sized floatation tanks on which she rides, are about to pay out as much as 1200 meters of cable at the end of which is a ten-tonne iron sinker and a mechanical butterfly, a device which will unfold, spread like wings and present a self-stabilizing sail to the current.

There's nothing new in this. In ancient times, mariners knew a counter-current flowed out through the Straits of Gibraltar, under the prevailing eastward set at the surface. Galleys would lower a sail weighted with stone deep beneath them to catch it, and be 'blown' out into the Atlantic. *Pelagus* was built to do the same, but the trick is in knowing where the currents are. The old fixed patterns have morphed with the chaos of the post-industrial environment, and we're building new charts as we go. Perhaps they will never be finished.

The atmospheric conditions for radio communications are never very kind down here. Only the station's high-power satellite dish, housed in a streamlined turret to protect it from the endless gales, can punch a signal through to the geostationary relay. We haven't known a truly clean transmission in my lifetime. Signal degradation is a fact of life, but if we can make the turn--heading north along the line of the Peru-Chile Trench instead of yet again plunging through the terrible seas of Drake Passage, south of Cape Horn--we'll find kinder air, and re-establish full signal load. Just to be able to talk to other human beings without husbanding bandwidth will seem like forbidden luxury.

*

15.00 hours comes around and you can hear a pin drop on the bridge. Grandmother is in the command seat she has occupied for 42 years. Her shock of silver hair is drawn back severely from a face etched with strain, but her eyes are piercing windows to a soul not yet ready to give up the fight.

There'll be little enough to see, but we'll *feel* it. We always feel it. A life in motion has tuned our middle ears to detect even the most subtle variations in the attitude of the station, and we all know what we're hoping to sense. The duty staff is joined by the off-duty watches and everyone who can pack in. There are now 202 Pelagians, and the station is crowded; every one of them wants to share the moment if they can.

The global chart has been expanded to show our position relative to Cape Horn. We're a thousand kilometers to the north, sailing down on the maze of islands lining the rugged southern coasts of Chile. We have no fear of grounding: the continental shelf of the western seaboard of South America is one of the narrowest in the world. We may actually see land. In the past, we've used wind power alone to come within a hundred kilometers of this latitude, but the surface currents never relinquished their iron grip on the station, taking her inexorably back into the jaws of Drake Passage. This time…it'll be different. I know it, I feel it. I *will* it.

The station's calculated position, based on a real-time sonar scan of the deep ocean bed beneath us, coincides with the projected maneuver point. A green circle surrounds the marker on the chart. My grandmother inclines her head to me with a tight smile. "You may give the order, Kira."

My voice sticks in my throat for a moment; the words take more effort to speak than anyone will ever know. I nod to the navigation officer and barely recognize my voice. "Deploy the sails," I whisper.

We see the indicators light as the winches slam into motion. Hundreds of meters down in the cold, crushing blackness, cable begins to pay out, and we wait, watching the strain gauges as the tonnage of steel beneath us descends. With three hundred meters of line out we start to move into the unknown. Every one of us is waiting for the tremendous shock that will race through the station if the cable snaps, taking our sails to the bottom. The more cable out, the more likely it is to break.

In my mind's eye, I see the sinker falling away into the alien realm: a space as total as anything above us, a space now populated only by jellyfish, siphonophores, arachnids and crustaceans. A terrible place where humans have never been welcome, made doubly so, in our minds, by the alienation of the surface world also. I hardly dare breathe as the strain indicators move toward the red zone.

It would have been a simple matter to probe the depths for this current set in the early days of the mission, but all the ROVs were lost long before I was born, and 3D printing new ones consumed too many resources. I asked a dozen times, but there were always more pressing needs to keep body and soul together for a growing population. Thus we stand now and wait. Many hug tight in the moment's tension.

I'm watching the tonnage indicator for the second the sinker passes out of the fresh water layer. When it enters salt water the greater density will reduce the downforce on the cable, and I'll know my theory was correct. Well, it'll *support* my theory--I'll not believe it until we're on a different course.

We're all scientists and engineers here. When the figures on the glowing displays change, a groundswell of relief runs through the bridge. We always knew the salt water was down there, but exactly *where* was the golden key.

"Target depth," the navigator whispers, and we see the hoist slow down gradually, finally locking off with 1020 meters of cable out. "Deploying the butterfly."

On a dozen screens a graphic builds up to show the sequence of the sails unfurling. When the confirmation comes that they're locked open, stabilizing vane fully extended, we hold our breaths. Five seconds. Ten. Fifteen.

Perhaps I'm the first to sense it, just by a second or so, but even 2° list is enough. The smile goes from face to face around the bridge as we each realize the station is tilting…angling in a way contrary to the press of the Convergence. This is the drag of the northward motion now filling the deep sails. The station is leaning to the south in response, and I nearly faint as the dashed gold line of our track on the big display deflects to the north-east.

A cheer like thunder breaks through the bridge. At once everyone is hugging and back-slapping, high-fiving, and it all grays out for me as my legs go weak. The next thing I know, my dad has caught me before I can collapse, and he's rubbing my back with words of reassurance by my ear. Someone thrusts a seat under me and I draw a shaky breath, my eyes never leaving the course projection. *Yes*, we have changed course. The pilot officer is trimming the upper sails, which are controlled by roller gear below the dome, to assist the new course. The station turns, stabilizes, wallows a little as the swells march by on a different angle, but we are definitely making headway across this infernal surface current.

Now, so long as the cable doesn't part, we're on our way.

*

Conditions are still far from good, but nothing will keep me from the landing pad. Dozens are out there at the safety rails, tethers trailing in the cold rain, but the sight is enough to take away our breath.

The late sun, on the second day after we made the turn, has found a gap in the overcast and its long rays paint the angry sea away to a horizon where, pink and gold in the evening light, stand the Andes. I've never seen mountains. I know these will only grow more impressive the further north we travel, but even now they hold me rapt. The dark ocean runs ponderously, but the wave crests are now lit in golden gleams, making them a wonder to my eyes, and the whole world seems pent with some expectation of new and better things to come.

Already I've put aside the fact I'm the one to see the possibilities in the equations, and to come to a conclusion unacceptable to others at that time. I've no idea what ego is, and no wish to learn. I stand with my father and grandmother, missing the mother who left us when I was young more than ever, and wishing she could have seen this amazing thing--the ranges rearing like the very walls of the world.

Night falls soon and the temperature will plummet. When we return to our closed habitat--to breathe the air of old Earth, to eat the synthesized, recycled food that's become the mainstay of human life--there is a sense of being at the beginning of a new adventure.

One day, I truly believe, I will see a blue sky.

Check out all of the Nomadic Delirium Press titles at:
http://nomadicdeliriumpress.com/blog/shop

If you've liked what you've read, please become a patron for Nomadic Delirium Press at
https://www.patreon.com/nomadicdeliriumpress

www.ingramcontent.com/pod-product-compliance
Lightning Source LLC
Chambersburg PA
CBHW071311130626
46556CB00004B/1562